CURIOUS

Larina's cheeks turned pink and her gray-blue eyes were now sea-green. They were always like that when she was angry.

"I want the truth, Sutton!"

"Darling, you'll have to bear with me, you'll have to trust me. Just for a little while longer. Then—then I'll tell you everything."

She shook her head. "No. Now."

"I can't!" he said angrily. "Don't you understand? I can't."

"No, Sutton, I don't understand. Call me stupid or whatever you want, but I don't understand. I have to know what's going on. I have to know!"

THE SEASON OF LOVE
An Arlene Hale Romance

Bantam Books by Arlene Hale

WHEN LOVE RETURNS
THE SEASON OF LOVE

The Season of Love

Arlene Hale

BANTAM BOOKS

TORONTO · NEW YORK · LONDON

A NATIONAL GENERAL COMPANY

THE SEASON OF LOVE

*A Bantam Book / published by arrangement with
Little, Brown and Company*

PRINTING HISTORY
Little, Brown edition published July 1971
Bantam edition published May 1972

For my niece, Kay,
my loyal and faithful reader.

I

ERNEST GOODWIN sat up with a start.

"Stella? Stella?"

The twin bed was empty. Groping for his slippers, Ernest groaned with a twinge of the arthritis that had been bothering him lately and muttered under his breath. Old age was for the birds, and although he ran ahead of it as fast and as hard as he could, it seemed determined to gain on him ever so slightly.

"Stella?"

"Did I wake you, dear?" Stella asked. "Sorry."

His wife was over by the window, a tall, regal woman whom he loved dearly.

"The wrist bothering you?" he asked.

"Oh, a little. I took another pill. No need for you to get up, Ernie."

"I'm awake now."

Pulling on a robe, he knotted it quickly and went over to the window to put an arm around his wife's shoulders. The cast on her wrist stood out white and heavy in the darkened room. Beyond the window, he saw the ripple of white caps on the ocean, the incredible smoothness of the white sand. He sighed. It *was* lovely here at the home they had long ago named Sea Mist. Gull Haven was a small but thriving Florida town on the Gulf Coast which, by some miracle, had not yet become a watering place for tourists. They'd lived here all their married life.

"Sure you're all right, Stella?" he asked.

"For the goodness' sakes, Ernest, don't pamper me so."

1

He laughed gently at that and rubbed his chin against her forehead.

"That's my girl. Always a little skittish under all the glamour."

"Oh, Ernie—"

He laughed again. They'd had a good life. A successful one. Tomorrow he would be making plans to go to Europe again. While he used to enjoy those jaunts to England and France, lately, they had become a little tiring. He supposed he should just retire, sit by the sea, and be an old man.

"I hate for you to go this time, Ernie," Stella said. Somehow, after nearly forty-five years of marriage, she knew what he was thinking.

"No word from Bert?" he asked.

Stella shook her head and took a moment to speak.

"No. Who knows when he will come this summer, if he comes at all."

"A strange breed, our son," he said thoughtfully. "Sometimes I wonder if I was to blame—"

"No. No. Neither of us. For some reason, God just gave us a son that was entirely different from either of us—"

Ernest Goodwin laughed. "Oh, I don't know. In my day, I was a bit of a rascal myself. Don't you remember—"

"Ernie!" she scolded.

Playfully, he kissed her and pulled her close, until she protested.

"You're acting the fool! Better come back to bed. I think I can sleep now."

"Run along. I think I'll stay up a little while."

She didn't argue. That was one thing about Stella. She had learned he was a man who liked to do what he wanted to do when he wanted to do it.

Pushing open the glass doors, he stepped out to their private little balcony that hung out over their carefully tended garden and looked to the Gulf beyond their sea wall.

It was one of those clear, open nights when sky and horizon blend together like an artist's colors. He breathed deeply of the salt air. He hated to leave on this trip. It had been a long time since he'd had any real time on the beach. Stella had her activities—her clubs and social gatherings—and there were the servants. Still he hated to leave her alone. Her broken wrist worried him. Stella wasn't a clumsy sort. Graceful. Like a queen. That was his Stella. But she *had* taken a fall and she *had* broken a bone. He'd feel better if someone were here with her while he was gone—family. Not Bert. He couldn't depend on Bert. Then with a grin, he thought of his niece, Larina. Sam wouldn't want to give her up, but he'd put up a fight for her. Larina and Stella hit it off. Always had. Larina could use the summer to paint. What better place than here at Sea Mist? He'd phone her tomorrow from the office, put the heat on, bend her arm, coax, wheedle, do whatever he had to do to get her down here.

That resolved in his mind, he began to feel better, easier. The company would be good for Stella.

He was about to go back inside when he noticed the light out on the water. A little odd. Too early for the fishing boats. Some pleasure cruiser, more than likely, making a night of it. The light blinked off, came on again, blinked off.

Signal? Some kind of signal? Ernie frowned. Kids probably. There were some strangers around. He'd heard they were going to open the old theatre farther up the shore. Put on summer plays. College kids. Probably just them, horsing around. Ernie grinned. He didn't begrudge anyone a little fun.

The light went on and off again. Turning away, he caught another answering light on shore. Or had he imagined it? Strange. He watched, senses keen, head up like an old fox. But there were no more lights. Sea Mist was ordinarily quiet; it seemed quieter than ever now. Just the surf rolling in, and a quickening of his senses that told him something might not be quite right.

Then with a shrug and a laugh at his imagination, he went back inside, closing the doors against the dampness of the sea air. Stella was already asleep. With a sigh, he kicked off his slippers.

Tomorrow he'd phone Larina. He was smiling as he

got back in bed. His only regret would be that if he could persuade her to come, he'd miss most of her visit. Larina was a sweet girl. He envied his brother Sam's good fortune in having her. Bert—well—Bert—he sighed. Bert was another kettle of soup. A rascally young man. Likable. Charming. But not worth a hill of beans. Why when he was Bert's age, he was already assistant cashier at the Gull Haven Merchant's Bank and on his way!

Ernie turned over and punched the pillow. He'd think instead of Larina. But that didn't work either. He fell asleep at last, the lights on the water blinking in his mind, on and off, on and off. Where had the answering signal come from? The summer theatre? Somewhere around the old Bleaker mansion? Hard to say. On and off—strange. Very strange . . .

Larina Goodwin was not asleep either. In her room, she watched the curtains wafting in the Midwest breeze and smelled blossoms from a tree. It was a soft, black night with stars scattered across the sky as if they'd been tossed aside by a careless child. The last school session had been more than two weeks ago. She'd cleared out her locker, her desk and the personal belongings in the art room and brought them home. In a rush of ambitious determination, she'd bought a supply of oils, pieces of canvas and splurged on a dozen camel's hair brushes. Every day, she would go out from the city of Riverdale and find a subject to paint.

"I'll keep faith," she said over and over again. "Things will work out. John will be back in the fall and we'll pick up where we left off. I know we will!"

But one thing had led to another and the brushes hadn't been taken out of the box, the new tubes of paint had not been squeezed open, and the canvas was just as white as it had been when she'd brought it home from the store.

She'd flitted from one thing to another like a restless butterfly. Her father was worried about her. In his gruff, attorney's way, he'd tried to talk to her about John.

"It might be best if you just forgot him, dear," he said.

"I can't do that!" she said, aghast at the idea. "John—well, he's special, Dad!"

Mr. Goodwin sighed patiently.

"Yes, I know how you feel about him. You think I'm just an old fogey, don't you? You think I've forgotten what it was like to be young and in love."

"It's wonderful!" she told him with a laugh. "Love knows no age, no season, no reason."

Then linking her hands behind his head, she had given him a hug and a fleeting kiss.

"Dear, why do you refuse to face this sensibly? John changed all your plans at the last minute. Took off on his own pursuits. I know how disappointed you were."

Larina frowned, remembering. She had been terribly disappointed. They'd made so many wonderful plans. But then, John had his point too. He had things he felt he wanted and needed to do.

"It will be all right when he comes back," Larina insisted. "You'll see."

Her father shook his head. "My poor little naïve Larina! I wish I had some of your blind faith sometimes."

"Stop worrying about me, Dad! I'll find a way to fill the summer. I've so many paintings I want to do."

"But I haven't seen you start one project." Mr. Goodwin looked at her from beneath his bushy brows. "John has hurt you, hasn't he?"

"It's all right, Dad! Really it is! Who knows, maybe the summer apart will be good for both of us."

"Well, if it opens your eyes a little bit to the truth about the man, maybe it will be worth it."

She laughed at that. "Oh, Dad! You're impossible, do you know that?"

"Yes, I suppose I am at that!"

The curtains of Larina's room stirred once again in the breeze and since she wasn't sleepy, she went to the window, knelt down and looked out to the dark night. The stars were so crowded in the sky. The midnight black was a perfect backdrop for them. With a sigh, she wondered where John was, what he was doing, what he was thinking.

She had dreaded the last day at Riverdale High,

where they were both teachers, for it meant not seeing
him again for nearly three long months. She had grown
so accustomed to listening for his steps in the hall, to the
way he popped through her classroom door with a smile
on his face. Then when he left, it was always in a hurry,
his footsteps clicking away down the hall.

It had been nearly the last day of school when he'd
told her of his change in plans.

"Listen, Larina, I'll be going away for the summer
after all."

"Going away! But you were going to stay here in
Riverdale. We were going to do so many things together—"

John ran a hand over his brow and gave her an
apologetic smile.

"I know, Larina. And I'm sorry. But things have
changed. I mean—well, I have some plans."

"Oh, Johnny!"

His long-fingered hands gripped hers for a moment.
There was misery in his brown eyes, a kind of begging
for forgiveness, a little boy's guilt. When he looked at
her like that, she couldn't deny him anything.

"Darling, I know this sounds crazy, but I need time.
Alone. I want to be sure about us. Absolutely sure. I
need this summer alone, to think things out, to sort of
search my soul, if you know what I mean."

"But I thought you *were* sure!"

"It will give you time too, Larina. For this one summer, we'll be free, no ties, no bonds—"

"But I like being bound to you, Johnny!"

He shook his head. "I want you to feel free, Larina.
And I want to feel free."

He had kissed her then. Very gently. It was the final
straw. She couldn't disappoint him, even when he had
disappointed her. If John felt he needed the time, then
he did. She trusted him. She wanted him to do what he
felt he had to do.

"I'll miss you, Johnny. Oh, I'll miss you so much!"

His grin was one of relief. Giving her a bearish hug, he
laughed. "You're a great girl, Larina. Almost too good to
be true. What can I say?"

"That you'll miss me too," she said.

"Every day, every hour, every minute," he told her.

Then suddenly the last day of school was upon them, John packed his things, said one last good-bye and was gone. The summer stretched out ahead of her, without John, a long, empty waiting.

But she was resolved to find a way to fill the summer. No matter what her father thought or said about John- ny, she trusted him, she believed in him. He hadn't simply given her the gate as her father kept implying. When he came back, their love would be sweeter, deep- er, and purer than ever.

She fell asleep at last on that thought. It was very late. The next morning, she heard her father get up at his customary time and soon there was the smell of coffee in the air. The phone rang. He answered it. She heard his voice rumbling on and on and she suspected there was some kind of argument. But she was too sleepy and tired to care. It was nearly noon when she got up herself, stretched lazily and felt sinful for having wasted so much of the day. Going downstairs she had just made herself a fresh batch of coffee when the phone rang again.

"Hello."

"Larina! My favorite niece!"

"Uncle Ernie! Where are you? What's wrong? Why are you calling?"

"Larina, didn't it ever occur to you that a long dis- tance call could be made just for fun, not for some kind of emergency?"

She laughed. "I guess not. How's Aunt Stell? Is her wrist all right?"

"She's fine and the wrist is coming along, slow but sure."

"Then what's wrong?"

"Nothing," Uncle Ernie sighed on the other end of the line. Will you let me explain? I want you to pack your things and come down for the summer. I want you to stay with Stella. I'm going to Europe in a few days. I hate leaving her alone."

"Do you have to go?"

"Afraid so."

Larina frowned. "You phoned earlier, didn't you? Talked to Dad?"

"Yes. I did. But he said you were sleeping and I didn't want to wake you up. I always forget about the difference in time."

"What did Dad say about this?"

"Well, he hates to let you come, but he thinks it would be good for you."

She bit her lip. What had Dad told Uncle Ernie about Johnny? It was hard to say, but whatever it was, she was sure Uncle Ernie had the wrong idea. Perhaps this was just a plot they had hatched up between them.

"Well, how about it?" Uncle Ernie asked. "Will you come? The beach is just waiting for you. You could do a lot of work down here. You always said you wanted to paint everything in sight."

She thought of the house they had named Sea Mist, that lovely place on the ocean, the sun-drenched beach and the old substantial homes so graceful along the shore. She knew a lot of the people there too and liked them. She had friends she'd made from other visits and it would be fun to see them again. Aunt Stella was very active in charity work and one of her pet projects was the Calley Home for Children. Larina had visited the place many times and been intrigued with it. Her trouble was that she fell in love with all the kids. She might be able to help Aunt Stella with the Home in some way and yes, in the far corner of her heart, she admitted to herself that it might help her get through the summer easier and quicker now that Johnny was gone.

"Are you sure you want me?"

"I want you and I need you. Stella is wild about the idea. She can't wait to start fussing over you. She always wanted a daughter, you know, and you're the closest thing to it that we've got!"

"All right. If Dad doesn't mind being a bachelor for the summer, I'll come."

"When can I expect you?"

"It would be fun to drive down. I'll have to get ready and it will take two or three days on the road—"

"Don't drive. Fly. I'll have a car for you to use here. Okay?"

"Uncle Ernie, I love you."

"Ditto." He laughed, pleased. "Let me know when your flight will be in and I'll meet you."

She hung up with a dizzy feeling. It had all happened so fast. Why hadn't she thought of it herself? Sea Mist would be perfect! She loved it there.

After a phone call to her father's office for a long talk with him, hearing the gruffness in his voice and his reluctance to let her go, but his love for her telling him it was the right thing for her, she began the hurry, scurry of packing. Gull Haven, Sea Mist, the children's home, the beach, the sun, the wine of the sea air—yes, it would surely make the summer easier.

She'd forgotten to ask about her cousin Bert. If he dropped around, it would be fun. She and Bert always had great times together. Perhaps because they were so drastically different. He never failed to shock and amuse her. Even if he was so irresponsible, he was always exciting to be with.

Perhaps, with a little luck, her summer would work out after all.

II

LARINA MADE CONNECTIONS with a jet flight the next morning and in a few hours, she had arrived in Florida. One more transfer and she was at the Gull Haven airport. The sunlight was brilliant. As she stepped down from the plane, she smelled the salt air. With an eager rush, she ran to meet Aunt Stella and Uncle Ernie. After a quick exchange of hugs and kisses, Uncle Ernie swept her away to the waiting car.

Nick Harper had driven them down and he had gone to fetch her luggage.

"How are you, dear?" Aunt Stella asked. "You look so thin!"

"I'm fine," Larina said. "I'm dying to see the beach."

She did hope they weren't going to ask her a lot of questions about John. She caught a glance being exchanged between them and knew that they had discussed this before meeting her.

"We want you to have a good time this summer," Aunt Stella said. "You don't know how much I appreciate your coming. I miss Ernie when he's gone for so long."

"How long will you be away, Uncle Ernie?"

Ernie shook his head. "I don't really know, Larina. Business doesn't always go as planned. I hope six weeks, maybe less. But more than likely, it will run into seven or eight weeks."

Larina linked her arm through his with a laugh. "You're getting to be quite an important banker, aren't you?"

"I keep busy. I make a little money, I lose a little. But

I manage to keep a roof over our heads. . . . What's keeping Nick?" Ernie added with a frown.

Nick had been with them for years. Ever since Larina could remember. His hair was snow white these days and his shoulders were stooped. His skin was tanned as brown as the straps on the portfolio she had carried on the plane with her. Nick's fondest memories were of the sea, and if anyone would listen, he would talk by the hour about his adventures on this freighter or that. Each year, they seemed to get more and more exciting and dangerous. She loved listening to him. Nick was in charge of the garden at Sea Mist and took care of the cars as well as the *Mary Belle*, a small cabin cruiser Uncle Ernie used for occasional relaxation on the Gulf waters.

"There he comes," Larina said. "At last!"

Nick was struggling under the mound of her luggage and the awkward length of her folded easel. Larina went to take it from him.

"Don't say it, Nick," Larina laughed. "I always bring far too many things."

Nick's leathery face crinkled with a grin that showed several teeth missing.

"Just like a girl. Me—all I need is my sea bag and I'm on my way. Possessions tie you down, Missy. Make a slave out of you. Me, I like to be my own man."

"Ah, Nick, you never change," Larina replied.

With Uncle Ernie doing the bossing, they got her things loaded into the sedan. Then with Nick under the wheel and Uncle Ernie in the front with him, they sped away from the airport. Larina found herself growing more and more impatient for the sight of the sea. It had been more than a year since she had last visited Gull Haven and she realized how much she had missed it.

"You know the first thing I'm going to do?" she asked with a laugh. "I'm going to take off my shoes and go barefoot on the beach!"

"You'll have time for a long walk before dinner," Uncle Ernie promised. "Matter of fact, I'll join you. I'll be leaving in the morning and I'll miss Sea Mist."

Larina devoured the surroundings as Nick pushed the

car along at a steady pace. Gull Haven seemed virtually unchanged and she knew everyone who lived there was hoping it would stay that way. So did she! It was just perfect as it was. Gull Haven was one of the few places still left in Florida that hadn't become commercialized. It was a peaceful, sunwashed place where a person could be as active or as lazy as she chose. There were a couple of good hotels and there were a few migrants from the North each winter, but for the most part, the beaches were private and the people who lived there were full-time residents.

Nick was not a fast driver and gave Larina time to get a good look at the familiar town. Then at last, they were turning down Beach Front Road and she saw the tiled roof of Sea Mist and the rolling surf, the incredible blue of the Gulf just beyond it.

"Oh, there it is!"

With a twinge of her heart, she remembered telling John about this place.

"I'd like to see it some time," he'd told her. "You make it sound like heaven."

"Heaven or a haven, whichever way you want to say it," she had replied. "Someday, I'm going to paint it all on canvas."

Remembering that now, she was glad to know that the urge to paint was weaving in and out of her veins with little streams of excitement. Since John had gone, all work had stopped and worse yet, so had even the desire. But now, perhaps, she would be able to do some really good paintings.

"The weather's been cooperating splendidly," Uncle Ernie told her. "Nice and warm, but not too hot. There's always a good breeze."

"Smell that salt air!" Larina said, gulping in great breaths of it.

Nick brought the sedan to a halt and before he could come to open the door, Larina had spilled out of the automobile. The house was gray, trimmed in black, large but neat. Nick's gardens were green and blooming, no small feat under the hot Florida sun.

"Your room's ready and waiting, dear," Aunt Stell

said. "Nick will bring your things later. Do you think you can take time for some cold lemonade? I told Bertha to have it ready for us when we came home. She'll serve it on the patio."

Larina really didn't want to do anything but rush down to the beach, but she didn't say so. The patio was a restful, scenic place that looked out to the sea and yet was fenced off so that it was completely private. There on a glass-topped, white wrought iron table, Bertha served them tall, slender glasses of pink lemonade.

"You're going to spoil me," Larina said. "All of you. It was so nice of you to invite me, Uncle Ernie!"

"I know you'll put some life into the place. I just hate it that I'm going to miss out. I think I'll plan on taking a jet home for a weekend or two—just to see what you're up to!" he said with a wink.

For a pleasant half hour, they talked of family and favorite memories.

"What about the children's home?" Larina asked. "How are things there? I've thought about it so often."

Aunt Stella shook her head. "In a bad way, I'm afraid. There are simply never enough funds. This summer, we must raise money. In fact, I've some committee meetings coming up next week to discuss that very problem."

"I'll donate some paintings," Larina said. "If that would help. I mean, if anyone would buy them—"

"That's sweet of you, dear."

"Oh, when I think of those poor, homeless little kids—"

"You were always taken with them, weren't you? There's a new child there you must meet, Larina. His name is Jimmy Baker and such an adorable little boy! But his story is so sad."

"What happened?"

"His father is dead. His mother was a drug addict. There was an overdose one day and, well—she died. The boy was completely alone. No family or known relatives. There was really no room for him at the Home, but they squeezed him in. It's enough to tear out your heart," Aunt Stella sighed.

They talked of other things, old friends and past good times. The lemonade was soon gone and the surf was calling. Larina could no longer ignore her desire to go walking along the water's edge.

Aunt Stella laughed. "I know you're dying to walk on the beach. Run along."

Larina hurried upstairs to her room and found Bertha had unpacked her things. Putting on a pair of sneakers and bright shorts with a cotton top, she rushed out to the beach. Uncle Ernie had been called away to the phone but Aunt Stella urged her to go ahead without him.

"He'll catch up," she said.

There was so much to see and absorb. To say the beach was lovely was inadequate. There were no superlatives in her vocabulary to do it justice. The only possible way she might be able to do so would be with canvas and oils.

There was a meeting of sky and water, white-winged gulls dipping and soaring, the beady eyes of the pelicans, the strut of sandpipers running along the sand ahead of her. The sun was yellow and hot, but the breeze was cool, tangy with salt. The sand was powdery white and had recently been swept. All the private homes along here had the beaches regularly raked and kept clean.

The urge to run came down on her and with a laugh, she flew along the water's edge, bare feet in and out of the surf as she rushed up the shoreline, her short black hair curling softly around her face. Then at last, she came to a halt and stood for a long while, catching her breath, staring out to sea.

"Well, hello!"

She turned. She hadn't noticed anyone nearby but now a young man was coming forward to greet her.

"Didn't mean to give you a start," he said. "You're staying with the Goodwins, aren't you?"

"Yes," she said. "I just arrived. I think I go a little mad when I first get my feet in the sand."

The man was brushing sand from his body. He was very brown, as if he'd spent hours in the sun. His hair was jet black and his eyes were gray. She had never seen him here before on her visits to Gull Haven. He was handsome and his smile was charming.

"I'm Sutton Ward," he said. "I moved in next door to the Goodwins. I happened to see you come from their house."

She laughed, a little embarrassed. "What you mean is, you saw me running like a maniac. I just couldn't wait to get down to the surf. I'm Larina Goodwin."

"I didn't know the Goodwins had a daughter."

"I'm not their daughter," she said. "Just a niece. But they're some of my favorite people. Do you know them?"

"No. I haven't met them yet. I hope to soon."

Sutton flicked the last of the sand from his swimming trunks and came forward barefoot to stand beside her and view the horizon.

"It's a very lovely beach, isn't it?" he asked.

"Beautiful. Just about my favorite place in the whole world!"

"I fell in love with it and the houses along here at first sight. Now, I'm living here and I couldn't be happier."

"Then, you're not a native?"

"No," he shook his head slowly. "Look!"

He pointed out to the sea and she saw the leap of a school of porpoise.

"Yes. You often see them," she nodded. "I love watching them. They're so graceful and playful."

She bent to pick up a shell and brushed the sand from it. It was a very tiny left-handed whelk.

"Are you a shell hunter?" he asked.

"I take them home by the boxful!"

Sutton Ward wrinkled his brow at her and smiled. His teeth were very white in contrast with his tanned face.

"Perhaps you'll teach me about them. I don't know one from the other."

"I'm usually out before the sun's up. If you want to join me."

He frowned. "Before the sun's up! You're kidding."

She laughed and gave her dark head a toss. "But I'm not. Oh, there's Uncle Ernie. Looking for me ... I have to run." She waved to him and ran toward Sea Mist.

Sutton Ward. The name was entirely unfamiliar but he was very attractive. She wondered what he did. There was no wedding band on his hand. She always noticed things like that. From all indications he spent a great deal of time on the beach. She would ask Uncle Ernie about him.

"Well, you seem to be having fun already," Uncle Ernie said.

"You know I go a little crazy when I get down here."

"Sunstroke," Uncle Ernie grinned. "I've told you to wear a hat! Have you had enough or shall we stroll some more?"

"More!" she laughed. "Of course! Let's walk down to the end of the beach."

She saw that Sutton Ward had disappeared. Linking her arm through Uncle Ernie's she asked about him.

"You've met him already?" Uncle Ernie said with surprise.

"Yes. He was on the beach."

"He spends most of his time there," Uncle Ernie said wryly.

"Who is he?"

"He leased the Bardwell place. Been here about six weeks. Other than that, I know very little about him."

Larina laughed and squeezed Uncle Ernie's arm. "You don't like him."

"I didn't say that."

"You didn't need to. I know you too well. I could hear it in your voice."

"Well, that's just between you, me, and that sea gull there. As a banker and a prominent citizen of Gull Haven, I try to be decent to everyone. Even slickers like Sutton Ward."

"Slicker?"

"Just my term for a man who lives high on the hog but has no visible means of support. How does he do it? Where did he come from? Why is he here?"

"He says he fell in love with the beach and the houses along Beach Front Road. You can't hang a man for that."

"Suppose not," Uncle Ernie muttered. "Never mind. I

shouldn't voice my opinion like that. I have no real basis for my dislike. Actually, he seems decent enough. I've seen him a time or two. At the hotel once and another time at the club, although I've never met him."

"You're just jealous, Uncle Ernie," Larina teased. "Because he's prettier than you."

Uncle Ernie snorted. "Handsome all right. A real ladykiller!"

"Well, I think I'd like him," she said.

Uncle Ernie swept a glance in her direction.

"*You* like everyone. Want to tell me about that scoundrel back home?"

"John isn't a scoundrel—no matter what Dad said."

Uncle Ernie patted her hand. "Okay, have it your way."

"I just want to paint, paint, paint and make the summer go by real fast. Maybe I can help Aunt Stella with the children's home too."

Uncle Ernie smiled, looking smug.

"I've got something to show you. I've been waiting for the right moment and I believe this is it!"

He took her hand and tugged her along, moving back toward the house. But instead of going inside, he walked toward the large, roomy garage.

"Isn't much, but it does have good light and it will be a cozy place for you."

"Uncle Ernie—"

The room had once been used as living quarters for a chauffeur, but Nick preferred the roomier area above the garage.

"Will it do?" Uncle Ernie asked anxiously.

The room was not large, but big enough. There was plenty of light, paneled walls and carpet on the floor. It had been furnished with odd pieces, but it was charming and she knew Uncle Ernie must have moved mountains in order to get it ready on such short notice.

"Your very own studio," Uncle Ernie grinned. "Okay?"

"Oh, Uncle Ernie! This is fabulous. How did you manage? How can I ever thank you? I've dreamed of having a place like this!"

"Maybe it will help the summer go quickly."

"Oh, yes! Yes!"

She moved to the window and looked out to the sea. She wouldn't think about John or how much she missed him or how bewildered she really was that he had gone away for the summer. Instead, she made herself concentrate on what she was seeing. In her mind the scenery took form and outlines started budding in her head. Color was waiting to be captured.

Yes, she'd paint. She'd work very hard. Somehow, someway, she would get through the summer and when it was over, John would be waiting for her!

III

By DINNER TIME, Larina had breathed enough sea air and soaked in enough of the warm Florida sun to feel her nerves begin to relax. She was almost groggy with fresh air. Bertha served a leisurely evening meal and topped it off with the delicious double chocolate cake that was her speciality.

"Ah, Bertha, I'll gain ten pounds while I'm here!" Larina said.

"You could use it, Miss Goodwin," Bertha replied.

Everyone laughed at that. Bertha had been with the Goodwin family for so long that she sometimes became a little bossy.

"How about a short cruise?" Uncle Ernie asked. "Nick is just itching to take the boat out."

"Will you come, Aunt Stell?" Larina asked.

"Yes. I will. Just to humor both of you."

Uncle Ernie rubbed his hands together. "Fine. Fine! I'll tell Nick we'll be ready to go in about half an hour."

They took their after-dinner coffee on the patio and as usual Uncle Ernie had to leave them to take a phone call. When he returned, he sat down with a sigh.

"That wraps it up. Everything's taken care of now and I should get off in the morning as planned."

Down at the private dock, Larina could see Nick busily fussing with the cabin cruiser, *Mary Belle*.

"You'd think that boat belonged to him," Uncle Ernie chuckled.

"He misses sailing the high seas," Larina said. "Don't you like to hear him tell about it?"

"Yes. Although I suspect his stories get stretched a little further every time he tells them."

The sun was dropping furiously red on the horizon when they walked down to the dock, kicking sand ahead of them. It was a lovely time of day on the Gulf. Color was everywhere, ranging from the deepening blue of the sky to the reds, pinks, goldens and oranges of the sunset.

Nick was jaunty in his faded sailor's cap. His bandy legs seemed shorter and more bowed than ever in the white cotton trousers he wore. With twinkling eyes, he gave her a hand aboard.

"It's a fine night for a cruise, Larina."

"That it is, Nick. Is the *Mary Belle* in good shape?"

"Never better. Gave the motor a good tune-up just a few days ago. Runs smooth as silk."

"Let's cast off, Nick," Uncle Ernie said.

Nick made a little ceremony of uncleating the mooring lines. Then with an important gesture, he twisted the key and the motor roared into life. With a spin of the wheel he turned the boat out to the open sea.

"Full throttle, Nick!" Ernie said with a grin.

The cruiser picked up speed. Larina felt the rush of sea air against her face and heard the bow slicing through the water. Aunt Stella had never been very fond of boats and she was trying hard to look relaxed. Uncle Ernie was delighted and kept shouting orders to Nick. They roared past fishing boats coming home from a day's work and small cruisers such as the *Mary Belle*. Far in the distance, they could make out the outline of a couple of tankers.

Glancing over her shoulder, Larina watched as Sea Mist grew smaller and smaller. Nearby, she caught sight of the white tiled roof of the Bardwell house and she remembered the tall, black-haired stranger she'd met on the beach.

For nearly an hour, Nick cruised about the Gulf, cutting fancy circles and giving the *Mary Belle* a full throttle. Uncle Ernie enjoyed every second as well as Larina. But poor Aunt Stell looked more uncomfortable by the minute.

"Uncle Ernie, maybe we should go back. Aunt Stella—"

"Yes," he sighed. "You're right. Okay, Nick, head it home."

Aunt Stell looked relieved.

Nick went more slowly back to shore. The white beach was pale and smooth in the twilight. An early star glowed. Larina noticed that no lights burned in Sutton Ward's house. Nick eased the boat to the dock, made it fast and helped them off. Uncle Ernie turned for one last look at the Gulf.

"I'll feast my eyes on it every day for you," Larina promised.

"Good! You do that. Keep Nick in line too, will you?"

Nick blustered at that and Uncle Ernie laughed. The two men were good friends.

"You just mind the banking business, Mr. Goodwin, and I'll mind the boat and the house," Nick retorted cheerfully.

"I'll be depending on you, Nick. Look after my two women for me."

They walked toward Sea Mist. When they reached the patio, Larina glanced toward Sutton Ward's house. Was he still on the beach or had he gone out?

"He's often away at night," Uncle Ernie said, as if reading her mind.

"Is he?"

"I take it that he's quite a man about town. I've heard him come home very late at night. Always hits the brakes too hard and makes the tires squeal. Just a bad driver, I suppose."

"He bothers you, doesn't he?" Larina asked.

"I'll admit that he does. Can't figure him and that always annoys me. I like to think I'm a good judge of men. But this one—"

Aunt Stella had disappeared inside. Larina and her uncle took comfortable chairs on the patio and spent the evening talking quietly. He was full of his business plans in Europe and he listened with care when she told him of some of the work she hoped to do here.

"Never could figure where you got your talent, Larina. Your father couldn't draw a straight line if his life depended on it. Or me either for that fact!"

"I'm just a stray on the family tree, Uncle Ernie."

"Maybe you inherit it from your mother's side."

"Perhaps."

"You never knew much about your mother's people, did you?"

"No," Larina shook her head. "Dad thought there were cousins in the West somewhere, but they're scattered. We've completely lost touch. It's sad to think about."

"Yes, I suppose it is."

Larina gave her dark head a toss and smiled. "But I'm lucky. I have Dad and you and Aunt Stella. And Bert. When I think about all those kids at Calley's, my heart just bleeds and I know how lucky I really am! Aunt Stella seems taken with the new little boy there."

"Most of them have sorry stories, but somehow, this one is especially pathetic. When you stop to think how drugs can destroy lives—"

"Yes," Larina murmured.

They fell silent, and Larina made a vow that she would help at the Home all she could this summer. Maybe she could even do something for little Jimmy Baker.

She stifled a yawn. The sea air was getting to her.

"I think I'll go to bed, Uncle Ernie. I'm incredibly tired."

"It's been a long day. You've come some distance since you got on that plane this morning."

"So I have! Good night."

She went inside and up the carpeted stairs to her room. There, she took a warm shower, put on her pajamas, and went to look out the wide windows across the end of her room. Aunt Stell had always given her this corner room, knowing how she loved the view. She could look to the sea or through the palms to the Bardwell house.

For a long while, she watched the sea as the surf rolled in and listened to the muted sounds of it. It was like music, lulling her to sleep. But strangely, she found that sleep was elusive that night. Finally, she got up and slipped downstairs. Careful not to awaken Bertha, whose room was just off the kitchen, she helped herself to a glass of milk. Then carrying it to the patio, she crossed to her studio. Snapping on a light, she walked about the room, planning where she would put her easel and store her paints and her canvas.

Oh, it was just perfect!

Draining the last of the milk, she put out the lights and went outside again. It was a warm, balmy night but the breeze against her face was cool and refreshing. Sutton Ward's house was still dark. If he didn't come home soon and get some sleep, he'd never make it to the beach for shell hunting early in the morning.

A furtive footstep on the flagstone startled her and she spun about.

"Who is it?"

"Oh, Larina! I didn't see you standing there."

"Nick? Is that you, Nick?"

"Yes, Ma'am. Just taking a short cut to my room."

"Where have you been so late?" she asked.

"Why—why I forgot to check something on the *Mary Belle*. Thought of it just a few minutes ago and thought I'd better get myself down to see about it."

"Oh."

"Goodnight, Larina. I—I hope you won't tell Ernie about this. I mean—I wouldn't want him to think I was getting careless or forgetful or anything."

"I won't," Larina laughed with a promise. "Good night, Nick."

Honestly, Nick babied that boat like it was a fragile, living thing!

Larina was about to go inside when she noticed a light flashing out on the water. Two flashes, a pause and then one more. Odd. What was it? Someone stranded? Perhaps they had motor trouble. Or was it just a fishing party? As she watched, she saw the lights flash once more. Then there was only darkness. Dismissing it from her mind, she went back inside.

With a yawn she climbed the steps to her room. She wondered what it was Nick had forgotten to do at the boat. He hadn't said. The minute her head hit the pillow, she was asleep.

Larina had fully intended to go shell hunting the next morning but with Uncle Ernie leaving for Europe, she joined him for an early breakfast instead.

Then a short time later, they accompanied him to the airport.

"Larina, if I'm needed for anything at all—for goodness' sakes put in an overseas call! Promise!"

"Yes. I promise!"

"Keep an eye on Stella for me."

"Gracious, Ernest, I'll be fine!" Aunt Stella protested. "I've only got a broken wrist and the cast will be off before you know it."

"Tut, tut," Uncle Ernie bristled. "I'm just looking for an excuse to come back, can't you see that?"

With a laugh, they waved him off and watched the jet streak skyward. They lingered until the plane was out of sight.

"Goodness, he is a worrier," Aunt Stella said lightly. "Little does he know that I rather enjoy these times he's away. I get a great deal done."

"Such as?" Larina asked.

"For one thing, I'll have the cleaners in. Ernest always hates any kind of disorder. I might even have the painters come. The house needs a fresh coat. Then there are a few little projects with Nick."

Larina linked her arm affectionately through her aunt's as they walked back to the car where Nick waited for them.

"You talk a good game, Aunt Stell. But I know how much you really miss him."

Aunt Stell sighed. "Well, at least, I have you, Larina. Thank goodness for that!"

"I wonder, would you mind if I had Nick stop downtown? There are a few art supplies I need. I didn't want to pack them all and bring them on the plane."

"Of course not. Make as many stops as you like. I'll just sit back and enjoy the ride."

The traffic was picking up in Gull Haven and business

them with backdrops, scenery, that sort of thing. It would be loads of fun, but something like that can take up so much of a person's time and I've so many things I want to do. I want to help you with the Home if I can while I'm here."

"That's sweet of you and I'll welcome your help," Aunt Stella reached over to pat her hand in a maternal way, "but I don't want you to feel obligated. Your uncle and I want you to have a nice time this summer. You're young and you're free. Enjoy the time while you're here."

Well, she'd see about helping at the playhouse. It would fill some odd, lonely hours no doubt, and she liked meeting new people. But first things first. She really *did* want to do some serious painting!

When Nick reached Sea Mist and opened the door for them, Larina decided to get busy at once. Changing into beach clothes, she filled her paint box with tubes of paint, selected a medium-sized canvas, snatched up her easel and headed for the smooth white sand of the beach. It was too perfect to stay indoors in her studio. Setting up her easel, she felt the hot sun scorching down on her. The surf rushed in to leave foam on the sand and then rolled out again. Eternally in motion. Coming and going, its tides pulled by the moon. Strange that the moon could do that.

With a piece of charcoal, she began to rough in an outline, sketching the dock and the *Mary Belle*, the expanse of beach and sky. In the distance, she would paint in a fishing boat as seen on the horizon.

She became absorbed. She was hardly aware of the hot white sand beneath her bare feet, the smell of the salt, the squeaky-hinged voices of the gulls. Just color, texture, form. They blazed in her head like the round yellow eye of the sun at noon.

"Hello."

It took a moment for her to realize that someone was standing at her elbow. With a start, she knew he had been standing there for several minutes. Turning about, she found Sutton Ward, dark glasses hiding his gray eyes, his brown shoulders covered with a bright sport shirt, his long legs trim and strong in a pair of blue swim trunks. His black hair was covered with a soft, canvas hat, the sort fishermen wore.

"Why, hello, Mr. Ward."

"Sutton, please," he said with a quick smile. "We are neighbors, you know. So, you're an artist!"

"Of sorts," she answered.

"I think it's great. I've always admired people who could do things like this. Me, I'm helpless when it comes to using my hands. I have no talent whatsoever."

He had managed to shatter her concentration. With a sigh, she wiped her brush clean on an old cloth and stood back to look at what she'd done. It wasn't bad. Not as good as it should be. But then, her work never completely pleased her. She was always striving to do just a little bit better.

"Are you a professional artist?" he asked.

"In a way," she replied.

"Forgive my curiosity," he said. "I'm really only trying to be friendly."

She glanced at him again, and he flashed that charming smile once more. There was something about him, distant and yet friendly, mysterious and yet open. She began to come out of the fog she was always lost in when she painted.

"You say you have no talent for painting. Where do your talents lie, Mr. Ward?" she asked.

He lifted his shoulders with a shrug. "Frankly, nowhere. I know a little about racing cars. A great deal about the casino at Monte Carlo. I've dabbled in real estate. I've also played the stock market. I once owned a ski lodge in Switzerland. Now, I'm here at Gull Haven."

"How exciting! Were you a friend of the Bardwells?"

"The Bardwells?" he asked. "Oh, the owners of the house. No. I don't know them. I leased the place through the realtor. I decided I wanted and needed a long, delicious summer on some private, uncluttered beach. What better place than this?"

"After Switzerland and Monte Carlo, Gull Haven must seem very dull and uninteresting. I'd love seeing those places."

His gray eyes gleamed. "Any place can be interesting

if you make it so. It is as they say about beauty. It is in the eye of the beholder."

She began putting the caps on the tubes of paint and placing them in order in her paint box.

"I've interrupted. I've ruined your mood. Sorry," he said, sounding very apologetic. "I didn't mean to be so—so—"

"It's all right really. It's lunchtime anyway and Bertha doesn't like to be kept waiting."

"Will you paint again this afternoon?" he wondered.

"Perhaps. Perhaps not. I'm a girl of whims."

"If not, would you join me at the country club? There's an excellent pool there. I've been doing quite a lot of swimming lately. Good exercise you know and—"

"That sounds like fun too, but I can't this time. Sorry."

Sutton folded his arms across the front of his gaily printed shirt and tilted his head.

"I'm being rejected?"

Somehow, she didn't know if he was kidding or not. He seemed arrogant and sure of himself. He seemed to serve no useful purpose to society whatever and somehow, she didn't like that. She knew she was idealistic and a romantic about many things, but the Goodwin family had never been rich enough to sit by the sea and while away their days. She respected men who earned their living by their own hands and brains. Although Uncle Ernie was comfortably well off, he still went to work every day at his bank. And her father kept long, busy hours at his law office. Perhaps Sutton was just one of the newer generation who believed in letting the world run itself without his help. If he was a rich man, maybe he was just lazy.

"Am I being rejected?" he asked again. "Unequivocally?"

She laughed. "Afraid so, Mr. Ward."

Besides, there was John. Even if he had pointedly made it clear that she was to be free this summer, she still felt bound to him. There would be no other men in her life. She was positive of that!

"Sutton," he said with a pained expression on his face. "Please, call me Sutton."

"All right, Sutton."

She folded the easel, handled the wet canvas with care, and reached for the paint box. Sutton was too quick for her. With a low sweep, he picked it up and tucked it under his arm.

"Let me help you. It's the least I can do for ruining your concentration."

He trod beside her, saying very little. She noticed that he walked with a rather hesitant gait. Was he lame? No. It was more that he seemed to favor his back. Or maybe the poor man had a sore foot. A person had to watch not to cut their feet on broken shells when going barefoot on the beach.

"The Goodwins have a lovely home here," he said as they approached the patio.

Bertha was preparing to serve lunch on one of the glass topped tables under the shade of a bright, striped umbrella. She was startled to see Larina with Sutton Ward in tow.

"Thank you, Sutton," Larina said. "You can put the paint box anywhere."

Aunt Stell, hearing voices, came to investigate. There was nothing Larina could do but introduce her to Sutton.

"I'm happy to meet you at last, Mrs. Goodwin," Sutton said. "I've intended to pay a neighborly call long before this."

"I'm sorry my husband isn't here, Mr. Ward."

"So am I. I should like very much to meet him. Perhaps I will, soon. I've seen him around town, but we've never been formally introduced. Your niece seems to be a very talented young lady."

With one wistful look at the lunch Bertha was putting on the table, he waved good-bye and began walking toward the beach. For a moment, Larina watched him go.

"Aunt Stella, what's wrong with him?"

"How do you mean?"

"The way he walks?"

"Back trouble," Aunt Stell guessed. "Your Uncle Ernie

had some trouble once and he walked just like that. Handsome, isn't he?"

Larina smiled. "I suppose he is. I didn't really notice."

Aunt Stell's wise gaze swung in her direction.

"Of course, you did! Any woman would. Even me! Ah, if I were thirty years younger—"

"Aunt Stell!"

With a laugh, they sat down at the table. Bertha served them an appetizing cool lunch that seemed a perfect balance for the hot summer day. The sun was different here. More direct. Yet it never seemed to leave Larina with a painful burn. She always tanned beautifully and her black hair would take on just a tinge of burnished copper.

"How did the work go?" Aunt Stell asked.

"Fine until Sutton interrupted. Want to see?"

"Of course."

Larina propped the partially painted canvas so she could see it.

"Hmm. Don't know how you do it, Larina."

"When it's finished, I'll have Tish put it up for sale in her shop. I'll donate the proceeds to the Home."

"You needn't do that!"

"But I want to, Aunt Stell. I really want to."

"Bless you, dear. Getting money for the Home is like squeezing blood out of a turnip these days."

"You're depressed."

"Yes, afraid I am. I know how the meeting will go next week. Just as they always go. Everyone has good intentions, but nothing ever really gets done."

"Then I'll have to be your spark plug!" Larina laughed.

They finished eating and the conversation turned to the next-door neighbor once again.

"Mr. Ward seems taken with you, Larina."

Larina made a mischievous face. "Poor man, I think he's just lonely."

Larina spent the rest of the day finishing the canvas. But she did not go to the beach again. Instead, she worked on the patio, consuming nearly a pitcherful of

Bertha's iced tea heavily laced with lemon, and working as if a demon were after her.

The painting wasn't very good, even though Aunt Stell said it was. She was still too intense, too wrapped up in yesterdays. Too many thoughts kept crowding in on her concentration, too many memories tugged at her. If anything good came out of the canvas, it was a kind of wistfulness, a longing, perhaps a loneliness. She missed John!

The next day, she dressed to join Tish for lunch and meet Lee Tyler. She chose a blue dress that brought out the blackness of her hair and blue of her eyes, that were at times green, at times gray, at times almost purple-blue. Uncle Ernie had given her the keys to a convertible that he occasionally drove and told her that she was to use the car as if it were her own.

It was fun driving along the palm-lined street. There were many royal palms here with their smooth gray trunks and umbrella tops of green fronds. Bright flowers bloomed along the houses, and the lawns, carefully watered and fertilized, were emerald green. Driving away from Beach Front Road, she left the shimmering blue of the sea behind her and pushed inland for a few blocks until she had reached the well-known eating place called the Red Lantern. Parking the car, she went inside. Tish spied her at once, and waved to catch her attention.

The carpeting was red and rich. The tables were polished walnut with captain's chairs around them. The air-conditioning was icy cold after the warm sun and music was muted, winging out over the room with low, relaxing tones. As she neared the table, the man with Tish Morgan got to his feet. He wasn't tall but he was well built with heavy shoulders, slim hips and a shock of thick, brown hair, decently cut. His eyes were hazel, perhaps moody.

"Larina, this is Lee Tyler. Lee, my friend Larina Goodwin." Tish made the introductions.

Lee Tyler smiled and it was a very warm, pleasant smile. For a moment, his big hand grasped hers. His touch was vibrant. This was surely a man with a great deal of personality and intensity.

"It's nice meeting you, Larina," he said. "I hope that between Tish and myself, we can persuade you to join our group. We need talent."

"I'm not at all sure I'll have time. I explained that to Tish."

"Well, we can discuss it later. Right now, let's have something to eat. This Florida climate has given me an appetite to end all appetites. Does a person ever get over it?"

"Sure," Tish said drily. "Maybe after four or five years. I'm a living example. I've gained fifteen pounds since I came here and somehow, the sea air just keeps making me hungrier and hungrier."

"You're becomingly plump, Tish," Lee grinned. "More for a man to love."

Lee ordered for them. He talked of his work at the college where he taught, of a few favorite students, of the plays he'd written and those he hoped to write.

"I regret that only a couple of them have ever seen the light of day on a stage. But this summer, I intend to use several of them. Unless, of course, the first one flops! Then we'll go back to the tried and true—"

"You make it sound like so much fun," Larina said.

"It is and it will be," Lee told her confidently. "We've begun renovating the old theatre. There's a tremendous amount of work to do just getting the place in shape before we can think about casting and rehearsals. Before you turn us down, Larina, why don't you drop by and give us a look?"

"Will you?" Tish asked anxiously. "There's some of us around almost every day."

Larina looked from one to the other. Then she nodded.

"Oh, of course, I'll drop by. I'll find the time somewhere."

"Good," Lee replied.

His eyes were very warm and friendly as they looked at her. In a way, there was something about him reminiscent of John. At the moment, she didn't know if that was good or bad.

V

LARINA WAS LIGHTHEARTED and gay. An eternal optimist. Finding someone so naïve was refreshing to Lee Tyler. He had not expected anyone like this. Funny how a man formed mental pictures of people just from a name or the way someone else spoke about them.

Larina Goodwin! As he ate, he listened to her voice and watched the color of her eyes change. One moment they were sea green, the next almost iris purple and then another, smoky gray. Somehow, he sensed when they were smoky gray, she was the most vulnerable. They were gray when she talked about Calley's Home for Children and the things she hoped to be able to do there to help. She positively glowed when she talked about the Home.

"They're great, all of them! Life's come along and dealt them a horrible blow and yet most of them can come up grinning when they see you. They've got courage."

Lee Tyler was fascinated with the emotions that crossed Larina's face, while Tish rambled on and on, telling Larina all about the players group. Tish pressed too hard sometimes. But that was her nature. She was open-hearted, spirited, dedicated.

The lunch was over much too soon. Larina got to her feet and told them good-bye.

"We'll be looking for you," Tish told her.

Lee nodded briskly. "Perhaps we'll see each other again, Larina. Gull Haven isn't all that big and I've claimed a room at the theatre for my own. Nothing fancy, but it will do for the summer. That almost makes us neighbors."

Then she was gone, leaving a clean, fresh scent of cologne. He watched her walk away. Not a very large girl. He liked that, not being tall himself. She moved quickly, decisively.

"Well, what do you think?" Tish asked.

"About what?" he wondered with amusement.

"Will she help us?" Tish asked. "Will she find time?"

"I don't know. She has too many plans for one summer. But I have a hunch she will."

Tish smiled. "Yes, so do I. Larina is a nice girl, Lee. She'd make a very enthusiastic member."

Lee paid the bill and walked with Tish to the parking area. Then waving good-bye, he climbed into his modest automobile and drove away from the Red Lantern. Flipping on the radio, he listened to the music with half an ear. When the newscaster came on, his attention was caught by the mention of Florida and the fact that in certain areas there was heavy dealing in drug traffic. The drugs were being smuggled into the state at unknown localities.

Lee frowned. Drug addiction was becoming quite a problem. As a teacher, he was acutely aware of it. He was also aware that the drug business was an incredibly lucrative one for the right sort of operator. According to the newscaster, several hundred pounds of heroin had arrived illegally in the state of Florida. Lee drove with sober concentration. His mind had left the newscast and gone to the play he had yet to finish. With luck, this afternoon he could find a few hours for some very serious work. It was a play he was especially enthusiastic about and he hoped he would see it come to life this summer.

Turning at last onto Beach Front Road, he pushed the Chevrolet along, the sea air blowing through the window against his face. Gull Haven was an incredible place. He'd heard about it quite by accident through one of his students. When he'd also learned of the old summer theatre that hadn't been used in the last five or six years, his interest had really come alive. Best of all was a working fund that had been lying dormant but drawing interest, just waiting for someone to come along and open the theatre once again. The funds were limited, but with hard work and some local support, he was sure he could replace all the funds and perhaps even add to them this summer.

Whistling, he caught a glimpse of the gray house trimmed in black where he knew the Goodwins lived. Tish had pointed it out to him. All along this road were nice, comfortable homes, some of them almost running to the plush side. But the farther he went up the shore, the smaller the homes were until finally he had reached the Bleaker house where it stood, old, majestic, and empty. It was just beyond it, rubbing elbows with the Bleaker property, that an old inn had been turned into a summer theatre.

Parking his car, he climbed out. He took a moment to look out to the sea, at the boats drifting there, the white-winged gulls stretching their wings against the sky. It was quiet, sun drenched, refreshing. If a man couldn't shake the cobwebs out of his head here, he was surely a hopeless case.

The old inn was a weathered gray. Paint hadn't graced its walls in a long time. In its day it had been a popular place, from what he could learn. The same people had come here, year after year, to bask in the winter sun and to rock on the front porch, to play bridge, and to take occasional excursions on the water. It had been a fashionable thing to do and people from the North had been quite possessive about it. Then the old inn had run into financial difficulties as the mood of the people changed and many of them found new, posh hotels and inns further south in the Miami Beach area. Then years later, someone had taken the trouble and time to make a theatre out of it.

"Now, it's my baby," Lee thought as he left the scenery of the Gulf and let himself inside.

The theatre had a seating capacity of a hundred and fifty. To the rear were small rooms jumbled with an odd assortment of props and backdrops. One of the rooms he had cleared out and taken for his own. Originally, it had served as an office. There, he made good use of the old desk, set up a folding cot, arranged some canned goods on a few shelves, purchased a hot plate and was established for the summer.

He had just settled himself at the typewriter when he heard the strange sound. With a frown, he pushed back from the desk. Then he heard the noise again, got to his feet and moved to the door. It was coming from the main room of the theatre. But he'd locked the door behind him when he had gone to the Red Lantern earlier and he hadn't heard anyone come in since he'd returned. How could anyone have got in?

"Hey! Who's there?" he shouted.

The noise broke off momentarily and then began again. Was he mistaken, or was it someone snoring?

"Hey!"

Following the sound, Lee went tearing across the room, bumping into the folding chairs. The snoring stopped and abruptly a red head poked up into view. Crew cut. Belonging to a man who looked twenty-four or so until Lee drew closer and then he saw that he was surely in his forties.

"Who are you and how did you get in here?" Lee demanded.

The redhead yawned, showing a bunch of white teeth, all of them capped. He was skinny, wearing a rumpled pair of slacks, a shirt open at the throat and sneakers. He needed a shave.

"Hi," he said, sticking out a hand. "I'm Hans Oliver, at your service. Better known as Nollie among my friends."

Lee ignored the hand. On instinct, he didn't trust this man. In the first place, how had he got in here?

Nollie yawned again and stood up undaunted. "You know, folding chairs don't make the best bed in the world. But I've slept on worse."

"What do you want?" Lee asked curtly. "How did you get in here?"

"Easy, fella. Easy. I haven't done anything wrong. I got here about eleven. Knocked on all the doors and windows and couldn't raise a soul. I've been hitchhiking for a couple of days and I was tired. I found a window that wasn't latched, so I let myself in. Took a little snooze—"

"Listen, Oliver or Nollie, or whatever your name is—"

"You the boss around here? You the fella that's going to produce the plays?"

Lee frowned. "Yes, I am."

"Hans Oliver, at your service," he said again, this time with a low bow. "I've played nightclubs, private parties, did bits in movies and off-Broadway. Do straight parts, leads, romantic cads, lovable bums, clown acts, debonair roles or if nothing else, I'll sell popcorn in the aisles."

Lee laughed. It was impossible not to. The man was some kind of nut.

Nollie held up his hand with a grin. "I'm star struck and have been all my life. Almost made it in the movies once, but I guess I haven't got the mug that makes women swoon. So, I've hit the summer circuit a few times. Now, here I am, at the Gull Haven Summer Playhouse. Can you use me?"

"You're not kiddding?"

"Listen, fella, do I look like I'm kidding? I need a job. I love the theatre. I don't know anything else. So, can you use me?"

"If you're looking for a money-paying actor's job—we work almost solely on a contribution basis. There just aren't funds to pay our actors—"

"Give me just a pittance, enough to eat on and keep body and soul together and couple of those chairs to sleep on and I'll do anything you want. Sweep floors, build sets, paint scenery, run errands, sell tickets, anything—"

The man sounded desperate. But there was a twinkle in his blue eyes that made Lee wonder if he was being taken in by some kind of con artist.

"I suppose I could spare a little from the working fund," Lee frowned. "I'll give you a trial. A couple of weeks. Then I'll decide whether you stay or not."

The hand came out again and wrung Lee's in a hearty grateful gesture.

"I certainly thank you, fella."

"The name's Lee Tyler."

"Nice to know you, Lee. Where do I hang my hat?"

Lee took a deep breath. "Anywhere you want, so long as you stay out of my hair."

"Gotcha!" Nollie laughed. "Hey, this is great! Beautiful weather down here. Never been here in the summer time. Played here once in the winter. Rained the whole time. But this is great. Listen, I think I'll take a dip in the surf. Want to come along?"

Lee started to shake his head. Then on second thought, changed his mind.

"All right, Nollie. I believe I will."

He found Nollie on the beach fifteen minutes later, a skinny, redheaded guy almost going berserk, running pell-mell into the surf. There, he splashed and shouted and cavorted like a small boy. His enthusiasm was contagious. Lee couldn't remember enjoying the Gulf as much as he did that afternoon.

Splashing out at last, they spread beach towels and basked in the sun. Nollie was a name-dropper. His tales and talk ran from the unforgettable Helen Hayes to Barbra Streisand, from Olivier to Mick Jagger.

"Nollie, how did you hear about the playhouse?" Lee asked.

Nollie rested his head on his hand, elbow bent and dug into the sand. "Believe it or not," he shrugged. "I read it in a paper in New York. Just a little item in one of the show-business columns. Somebody must have heard about it, printed it, and here I am!"

Lee frowned. Odd. Gull Haven was not well known and certainly no one in New York could be interested in the old playhouse. But then he supposed some writer was hungry for material and had used whatever he could find.

"Hey, want to hear me do Shakespeare?" Nollie asked. "*King Lear?*"

Lee grinned. This guy was a nut! But refreshing too. Just the sort of general, all-around know-it-all that they could use this summer.

"Okay, *King Lear*. Go!"

Nollie began spouting Shakespeare and Lee had resigned himself to being bored. But surprisingly, Nollie

---

afternoon wa
waited. Ther
very vital a
solve it by
"Listen
"Sure
quiet,
straig
salv
a

EW DAYS, Larina painted fo
rying very hard to lose herse
ly she took her easel to the beach,
e she used her new studio. She hadn
d again. Perhaps he was away for a few

t herself going stale, she covered her
Aunt Stella that she wanted to visit
r Children.

k—"
ak!" Larina told her. "Besides, you've
bout little Jimmy Baker that I'm dying

this morning," Aunt Stella promised.
as about twenty minutes away from
ad. Driving there, Larina remembered
e had visited. She had come to know
dren there. Of course, some of them
ow. It had been over a year since she'd
But there were always a few that got
ound adoptive parents or even a foster

for a novel idea to raise money," Aunt
f you can think of anything—pass it

med shabbier than ever. Even Larina's
es saw that the place badly needed
dren were outside, playing, and when
nvertible, they stopped to stare. But
familiar sight there and they knew she

44

spoke with a great deal of eloquence and dramatic effect. Lee became absorbed.

When Nollie had finished his scene at last, Lee stared at him.

"You're for real!"

"Didn't you think I would be?" Nollie asked. "Just never got the breaks, man. That's all."

"I believe we'll be able to use you, Nollie."

"I'll earn my keep. That's a promise," Nollie said. "Say, you know, things are beginning to look up for Hans Oliver. Yes sir, they surely are."

Nollie went from Shakespeare to Arthur Miller to William Inge to Thornton Wilder's *Our Town*.

When he broke off at last, there was a frown on his face and his gaze was directed down the beach.

"Who's that?"

Lee glanced over his shoulder. The man was tall, had black hair, wore sunglasses and walked in a stiff-legged sort of way.

"Lives around here I think," Lee replied. "Down the beach. I see him walking along here often."

"Yeah?" Nollie asked. "What's his name?"

Lee shook his head. "I don't know. Never met the man. I haven't been here very long myself."

"Funny. Looks familiar somehow. Wonder where I met him?"

"Who can say about that?" Lee asked lightly. "You've been everywhere, done everything, met so many important people—"

"You're right," Nollie grinned. "Just my imagination."

The man had spotted them. He paused, bent to pick up a shell, gazed out to the horizon for a moment, and then turned back. Funny. He always walked on past the theatre, and followed the beach to the old dock before turning back.

"Friendly cuss, isn't he?" Nollie asked.

"Believe it or not, Nollie, there are a few people who don't run off the head to everyone they meet."

"Meaning I do?" Nollie asked with a grin. "Sorry. It's just me bloomin' personality."

Lee got up to brush the sand from his trunks. The

gett
e was
d givi
olling ab
anything
Lee said.
f you want t
ntened and cl
ageable that we
Sure thing, Lee
other snooze. Ma

Lee nodded and
he glanced back. N
was up and walki
sunglasses at a dis
man like Nollie wh
or what he did o
them?

Then with a sh
business and went

FOR THE NEXT F
cated sessions,
work. Occasiona
most of the tim
seen Sutton War
days.

When she fe
easel and told
Calley's Home fo

"But your wor
"I need a bre
talked so much
to see him!"

"We'll go over
The Home w
Beach Front Ro
the last time sh
most of the chi
would be gone n
last been here.
left, who never
home.

"We're looking
Stella sighed. "
along!"

The Home see
inexperienced ey
repairs. The chil
they saw the c
Aunt Stella was a

was not a prospective parent, so they went back to their noisy games.

"Over there," Aunt Stella said. "By himself. He's still a little withdrawn. Doesn't join the others very much. Come along, Larina. I'll introduce you."

Jimmy Baker was about six, with brown hair, large brown eyes that could melt Larina with just one look, a dirt smudged, pale little face and expressive hands. His shoulders were rigid and his eyes suspicious.

"Hello, Jimmy," Aunt Stella said. "I've brought you a new friend. This is Larina."

"Hello, Jimmy," Larina said.

"I'll leave you two while I go inside," Aunt Stell said.

Jimmy was leaning against an old pine tree, hands stuffed into his pockets.

"Don't you like to play games, Jimmy?"

"No!" he said crossly.

"Oh. Well, in that case, let's go for a walk."

"No."

"Please? With sugar and cream?" Larina asked.

She gave him a smile and he stared at her for a moment with huge, brown eyes.

"No."

Larina shrugged her shoulders. "Okay. I didn't really want to go anyway."

He was watching her carefully. Larina picked up a stick and began scratching in the sand, making a picture of a round faced boy with a sad mouth.

"Sad Jimmy," Larina sighed. "That's what we'll call him."

He was getting curious. After a moment, he edged a little closer for a better look.

"Shall we change him?" Larina asked.

Jimmy didn't answer. She paid no attention, but drew another face in the sand and this time, added a big smile.

"Oh, that does something for him, doesn't it?" Larina asked.

Jimmy stared at the sand drawing, keeping his hands in his pockets.

"I draw pictures. Lots of pictures. Someday, maybe I'll make a painting of you. Wouldn't that be fun?"

"Maybe."

She laughed and gave her dark head a toss. Then reaching into her pocket, she held out a closed fist toward him.

"Present. Go on, take it."

He held back. She wiggled her fist. "It won't bite," she promised.

Finally, he extended his hand and she dropped the gift into his small palm.

"It's a seashell," she said. "I found it on our beach. Isn't it pretty?"

He fingered it, turning it over and over, examining it from all angles.

"The next time I come, I'll bring you a great big one. You can hold it up to your ear and hear the sea in it!"

"Oh."

She laughed again and reached out a hand. For a moment, he seemed to shrink back.

"Oh, Jimmy, I just want to be a friend. Okay?"

"Never had a friend."

"Well! You have now!"

This time, he allowed her to touch him. She grasped his shoulders in her hands and tugged him closer. She could see the golden specks in his brown eyes and the texture of his thick hair.

"Do you like dogs?" she asked.

He nodded his head.

"I saw a nice little pooch on our beach the other day. Maybe if you come and visit sometime, you could play with him."

"When?"

She laughed and ruffled his hair. "Well, soon. I promise. It will be soon."

During the short time she was there, she urged him to take part in some of the games the other children were playing. He would do it only when she joined them herself. So for a vigorous thirty minutes or so, while Aunt Stell was busy inside, she played tag, hide and seek, and London Bridge is falling down.

Then at last, it was time to go. Jimmy followed her to the car.

"Good-bye, Jimmy," Larina said. "I'll see you soon."

"When's soon?" he asked.

She brushed back his hair from his forehead and looked into the brown eyes. Her soul was lost in that moment and she knew it. Her trouble was that she couldn't resist children like this. She was always too softhearted about everything.

"Not tomorrow. But maybe the next day. Whenever I can, I'll come. Okay?"

He nodded vigorously.

"Still have your shell?" she asked.

He dug eagerly into his pocket and found it, holding it up for her to see.

"Keep it," she said. "It will be like a promise in your pocket." Then she gave him a brief hug and climbed into the car. He waved and was still watching them as she looked back for one last time.

"How do you do it, Larina?" Aunt Stell asked.

"Do what?"

"Melt down little boys like that? Do you know he's been very withdrawn ever since he came. Yet, just a few minutes with you—"

Larina was secretly pleased. She laughed and blinked back tears at the same time.

"Oh, I don't know. We just communicated some way. I think kids sense things. He knew I liked him on sight."

"Ah, Larina!" Aunt Stell laughed. "You're so quick to love!"

"Who couldn't love a little boy like that?" Larina wondered.

Aunt Stell frowned.

"I suppose his mother *did* love him. I don't know."

The effect of being with Jimmy stayed with Larina for a long time. It was never completely gone, but lingered in the corners of her heart. Sometimes, working at her easel, she would pause and look out to the sea, thinking about Jimmy. Somehow, it brought the problem of drugs and their users closer to home.

After a particularly busy and tiring day at the easel,

she decided to go for a swim in the Gulf. The beach was sloping and the tides were predictable in this area. Even though there was no danger swimming here, it always seemed to be a challenge to Larina. It was fun to pit her strength against the oncoming waves, to swim away from the shore into the infinitive expanse of blue water.

She swam for nearly half an hour until she began to feel tired and relaxed. Splashing out, she spread a beach towel and stretched out to dry in the sun.

The sun made her drowsy and she must have dozed, for when she opened her eyes, the sun was blotted out and she realized someone was standing over her, between her and the sun. For a moment, she blinked.

"Hello."

Sutton Ward!

"You know the story about the proverbial bad penny," he said in his low, pleasant voice. "Here I am again. I thought of waking you but you seemed so peaceful."

"I was," she laughed. "I was drifting with the tide."

He smiled at that. Then without invitation, he sat down beside her on the sand, stretching out his long, brown legs. She had never seen him in anything but swimming trunks and she wondered in a curious way how he would look in a suit and tie.

"Tell me, Larina, are you interested in the summer theatre they're opening up this summer?"

"I'm a little curious," she said. "Why? Are you?"

"I've walked up there a few times. Activity seems to be picking up. It must be fun. I've—I've never had the opportunity to join anything like that. Do you suppose they could use a man like me?"

This surprised her. Sutton Ward hardly seemed the type.

"What talents do you have? Would you be another Barrymore?" she teased.

He laughed and his white teeth flashed. She wished he weren't so good looking.

"As I told you before, Larina, I have no talent. But perhaps there would be something I could do."

"You hardly seem the sort—"

"I enjoy life, Larina. I like poking my nose into new

things. Frankly, I've been a little bored here. After the first few days of soaking in the sun, I began to get restless."

"Does that mean you'll be off to Monte Carlo or some other exotic place?"

He shook his head quickly. "No. I'll spend the summer here, as I planned. Do you know anyone connected with the playhouse?"

"Yes. I'll pass the word on if you like. I'm sure they'll contact you."

"I'd be most grateful," he said. "Thank you."

He pulled his legs up and wrapped his arms around them. The sun made his black hair seem glossy and his eyelashes were thick and long. But probably his most fascinating feature were his gray eyes. Cool one moment, hot the next. There was a shrewd intelligence to the man.

The surf came crashing in and she watched the rollers breaking, making the *Mary Belle* rock where it was moored at the dock.

"We're going to get caught in the next few minutes," he laughed. "The tide's coming in."

"I should be getting back anyway," she answered.

She got to her feet and he leaped up at the same time. Then with a gasp, he put both hands to the small of his back and bit down hard on his lip. His face was contorted with pain. His gray eyes were abruptly dull, all light gone out of them.

"What is it?" she asked with alarm. "What's wrong, Sutton?"

"Sorry," he muttered. "I—I have these spasms occasionally. I—I hate to ask, but would you help me home?"

She nodded. "Of course. Oh, dear, is it bad?"

"If you'd just let me lean on you, I think I can manage it."

His arm draped heavily around her shoulders and he began walking, partially stooped, his face white and breaking out with perspiration.

"Should I call for help?" she asked.

"No. No. Please. I'd rather you didn't. I'm a little

sensitive about this. I—I suppose no man likes to have trouble navigating on his own. I'm sorry it had to happen in front of you—"

"Don't talk," she said. "Just concentrate on getting to the house."

His steps were labored and his weight was becoming unbearable. The poor man! She wished there was more she could do!

"Serves me right," he muttered. "I should never leave the house without my capsules."

They were nearing the Bardwell house at last. He looked with anxious longing at the chaise longue on the patio. With one final effort, he stepped up to the stone floor and with care, she helped him ease down to the chaise.

"Lie back," she said. "Rest. You're exhausted."

"My capsules—they will help immensely."

"I'll get them for you, if you'll tell me where they are."

"My bedroom. On the bedside table. First door to the right off the hall. Please, hurry—"

She fled into the strange house. She had never been inside the Bardwell house before. She found it to be very luxurious, tastefully furnished, and spotlessly clean. It was almost as if no one lived here. It took a few moments, but she located the bedroom. The bottle of capsules weren't where he said they would be.

Glancing about, she spied a jacket hanging on the back of a chair. He was probably in the habit of carrying them with him. Without a moment's hesitation, she thrust her hand into the pockets. There was something hard and heavy in the inner breast pocket. She felt it swinging there as she tried first one side pocket and then another.

"There!" she said triumphantly.

The vial was half filled with white capsules. Rushing back to the patio, she went to bend over him. He was lying very still, with his eyes closed. She put a cool hand to his forehead.

"Sutton—"

He stirred. "Thank you. You found them. There's a pitcher of water over there on the table."

She filled a glass and brought it back to him. While she watched, he swallowed two of the capsules.

"Are you going to be all right?" she asked anxiously.

"Yes. In a few minutes. Larina, I'm sorry to be such a bother."

"It's all right, but you gave me a fright! Do you often have these spasms?"

"Yes. But I've been told they will pass. I—I had some surgery a few months ago. I suppose I might as well tell you. That's really why I came to Gull Haven. It's a quiet place and I needed rest badly. Give myself time to heal."

"I see. What a shame! But if any place can help surely it's Gull Haven."

"Most of the time, I'm quite well. But having a tricky back can be a problem," he admitted.

She sat down opposite him. Somehow, seeing him like this, he no longer seemed so arrogant and cocksure. In a way, she liked him more for it.

"Funny," he murmured. "I had hoped to impress you, to perhaps have you as a guest in my house. Now, you're here—and I'm flat on my back and being a nuisance."

She laughed. "It's quite all right, Sutton. You do have a lovely house. Are you here alone?"

"Yes. I have a woman that comes in twice a week to clean, do the laundry, and things like that."

"It's a big house for one man."

"I'll grant you that. But I never liked being cooped up, Larina. Always needed space."

"Are you feeling better now? Could I get you anything else?"

He shook his head and gingerly sat up. Running a hand over his black hair, he gave her a careful smile.

"No. The capsules are working. They're fast. I'm glad of that."

"Do you think it's wise to be here alone?"

He looked at her for a long moment. "Yes. It's all right. Perhaps I overdid the swimming this afternoon. The Gulf waters were recommended to me and they have relieved the soreness tremendously. But I do limit myself to a few minutes at a time. Gradually, I'll work up to longer periods in the water."

"It's like therapy?"

"Yes, that's a good word for it, Larina. So, I've become sort of a beach bum. The sun has restored my energy too."

He seemed to be getting over his painful seizure and when he said there was nothing more for her to do, she said she should be getting back.

"I wish you'd stay. Keep me company."

"It's getting late. Bertha will be expecting me for dinner. Aunt Stell's going to be away and I told Bertha I'd eat early tonight. That way, she can have the evening free—"

Sutton smiled at her. "You're a very thoughtful girl. In fact, why don't you stay here?" he asked again. "Say, can you cook?"

She laughed. "Of course I can cook! I always cooked at home and especially after Mother died."

"I can't. I'm horrible in the kitchen. Sometimes I phone and have my meals delivered. I can manage some pretty bad coffee, but not much else."

She began to see what he really wanted. She was amused and surprised. But why not? The poor man was ill. Like so many men, he was helpless when it came to preparing food.

"You want me to stay and make dinner?"

"Would you?" he asked hopefully. "For the two of us."

"I'd like to help, but—"

"Good! Then you'll stay."

Sutton seemed so eager. Like a hungry, lost boy in need of help.

"All right," she laughed. "What would you like?"

"Anything. Just anything. If you can't find it in the kitchen, I'll get it," he said, his face lighting up.

"You might be sorry," she told him. "I'm not a gourmet chef."

There was one pause on the way to the kitchen to phone Bertha that she would not be there after all. The kitchen was modern in every way. Inside the huge refrigerator, she found ample supplies. With Sutton perched on a step stool, she tied a dish towel around her waist and went to work. Soon the fragrance of broiling steak filled the air. Sutton leaned against the counter, watching with his gray eyes. His color had returned and he was able to walk upright again.

"Steak is my father's favorite," she said.

"Your father? Where is he?"

"Home in Riverdale. An attorney. I feel a little guilty coming here for the summer and leaving him alone."

"But we do have to live our own lives, don't we?" he asked quickly.

She met his gray eyes. "Yes, I suppose we do."

"I believe these days they call it doing your own thing," he said with a smile.

"Yes," she laughed. "What about you? Don't you have any family?"

"Not much," he replied carefully. "At least, I seldom see them."

The percolator was bubbling and when it stopped, Sutton got up to pour the coffee.

"Everything's ready but the toast," Larina said. "Do you like it light or dark?"

"In between. Shall I fetch the trays? We could eat on the patio. I must say the sunsets are worth watching."

"It's an hour until sunset," she answered.

His gray eyes glowed. "I know. But we could wait for it, couldn't we?"

She didn't reply to that. But when he brought the trays, she arranged the two plates of food on them and he carried them out to the patio. It was comfortable there. Perhaps a bit more private than at Aunt Stell's and it looked toward the far end of the beach. She could even make out the roof of the Bleaker house.

Sutton devoured the food hungrily.

"Why don't you hire someone to fix your meals?" Larina asked.

He shook his head quickly. "No. I'd rather not have anyone around. I'm peculiar that way. I—I'm not an easy man to live with. I keep irregular hours. I'd drive a cook crazy within a week's time."

They laughed at that. Larina was aware that she had

come to like Sutton Ward. At times he was amusing as
well as polite and thoughtful. He seemed genuinely
pleased with her company and it was the kind of attention that could turn almost any woman's head. He was so
totally different from John and she'd never known anyone like him before.

"Paint me a view of this, Larina, and I'll buy it,"
Sutton said with a sigh. "It is a very beautiful beach."

"But there are so many beautiful and interesting places in Florida."

"I haven't seen many. Perhaps someday, soon, I'll go
sight-seeing. I'd like to visit Tarpon Springs. They gather
sponges there. Should be interesting."

"Yes," she nodded.

"Would you come with me?" he asked in a quiet,
hopeful voice.

"Who knows," she said. "I follow the wind!"

"Maybe you're just being a cautious young lady."

She felt the smile fade away from her face. Now, he
was getting on dangerous ground, beginning to press too
hard. Getting to her feet, she told him that she had to be
going.

"So soon?"

"Yes."

There were footsteps inside the house. With a start,
Larina turned about. A man stood there, partially in the
shadows so that she couldn't see his face. Sutton leaped
to his feet and his expression changed. All the warmth
and charm was gone and was replaced with a cold
hardness.

"I'll be with you in a moment," he said curtly to the
intruder. "Please, wait inside."

Why was Sutton acting so strangely? Who was the
man standing in the shadows and how had he got inside
the house?

"Sorry," Sutton was saying.

He took her by the arm and walked with her to the
edge of the patio.

"Thank you for everything, Larina. I'll see you tomorrow. On the beach. For shell hunting in the morning. All
right?"

Then with a nod, he turned away. She stepped down into the white sand. She had just been given the bum's rush and it had surprised her. Sutton had been so warm and charming only a moment ago! Glancing back, she saw him walking swiftly toward the door. For the first time, she noticed the little white scars just above the band of his swimming trunks. He said he'd undergone surgery. Yet, the scars didn't look like an incision a surgeon would make.

Puzzled, intrigued, and more than just a little curious,. she walked through the sand toward Sea Mist.

"Yoo-hoo, Larina!"

Someone was calling to her. With a wave of her arm, she saw Tish Morgan waiting for her.

"What were you doing over there?" Tish wondered with a curious expression on her pretty face.

"You'd never believe it!" she said.

"Sutton Ward lives there, doesn't he?"

"Do you know Sutton?" Larina asked with surprise.

"He's been in my shop a time or two. Handsome devil, isn't he?"

"Yes," Larina admitted. "What do you know about him, Tish?"

"Not much. Listen, I'm on my way to the playhouse. Why don't you come along."

"Why not?" Larina said.

VII

A short time later, Larina, dressed in a green dress of a soft, cool material, joined Tish.

"So, all right, when do you tell me?" Tish wondered as they drove away from Sea Mist.

"Tell you what?"

"What you were doing at Sutton Ward's house!" Tish said with exasperation. "Honestly, don't you know he's just about the most eligible new man in Gull Haven? There are several women I know who would give their eye teeth to get inside his door!"

Larina laughed. "Oh, really, Tish. He's just an ordinary man. A little lonely and a terrible cook. I fixed some steak. He ate as if he was starving!"

"Larina Goodwin, you amaze me. You sound as if that's something you do every day!"

"Well, I usually cook for Dad."

Tish shook her blonde hair and turned her attention to her driving. It didn't take long to reach the far end of the beach. Soon, they were going past the Bleaker house.

"Such a shame about that place," Larina said. "I imagine it was once a very lovely home."

"Yes. I never could understand why they just let it stand. No one lives there. Can't they rent it or sell it?"

Larina shook her head. "As I understand there's some kind of legal snarl that's been dragging on for years. Meanwhile, the house just sits there and grows older."

"Sort of spooky, isn't it? A perfect setting for ghosts."

"If you believed in them."

"Knowing you, I'm surprised you don't!" Tish teased.

Whisking past the Bleaker house, they soon saw the old inn that had been made over into a summer theatre. Tish brought the car to a bouncing halt.

"Sounds like some activity inside," Tish said.

"Either that or they're tearing the place down!'"

The old inn had once been a popular place in Gull Haven, although it was before Larina's time. Uncle Ernie had told her about it. Now, the place could seat about a hundred and fifty people. The stage was not large, but adequate. A red-haired, wiry man was busy working on some old props, wielding a hammer with a savage determination.

"Hi," Tish called. "Where's Lee?"

"In his office," came the reply.

Lee heard their voices and came out. There was a harried look on his face as he put a pencil behind his ear.

"Well, hello," he said.

"How's things going, Lee?" Tish asked.

"Slow. Much too slow. If we're not careful the summer will get away and we won't have nearly enough plays produced." ·

"We go into rehearsal next week, don't we?"

"Yes. If we can just get the sets ready and the props gathered up."

"New volunteer?" Tish asked nodding toward the red-haired man.

Lee smiled. Larina noticed how it lighted up his hazel eyes.

"Come along. I'll introduce you."

It was Hans Oliver, who immediately explained that everyone called him Nollie. Nollie and Tish seemed to get along especially well.

"Could I show you around, Larina?" Lee asked.

Larina nodded. "I'd love to see it. I've been here but I'd forgotten what it really looked like. Do you expect a good season?"

Lee grinned again. "We always hope, don't we?"

He took her into every room at the theatre and she saw all the dusty old props and the backdrops with their faded paint.

"You can see why we need your services, Larina," he explained. "We'll be starting to work on these in the next day or so. The plan is to rehearse a couple of hours every evening and then spend the rest of the time working on the sets."

"What do you need?"

Lee's eyes flickered. "You mean, you'll help us?"

"I'll do what I can. It looks like fun. I've never been involved with anything like this."

"First we'll need a country scene. All of the first act takes place there. Then an interior setting. I think we've got enough decent stuff to use for that. The last act calls for a railroad depot."

"I see."

Lee took her arm and guided her into the last room which at one time had been an office. Now she saw that he had fixed it up as living quarters. The desk was filled with sheets of paper and the typewriter stood there waiting like some dark animal about to pounce.

"You've been working. We shouldn't have interrupted."

"I let Nollie talk me into going for a swim this afternoon so I got behind," he replied. "But I was more than ready for a break."

"What's the name of your play?"

"*The Way of Love.*"

"Sounds interesting," she said with a teasing smile. "Writing from experience?"

His hazel eyes met hers. Then he gave her a quick shake of his head. "No. Not really. There's never been a girl I was really in love with. Oh, there were a few school crushes, you know the bit—"

She thought of John. There had been nice boys in high school. Nicer ones in college. But there had never really been anyone in her life until John Adair. He had come on with a rush that left her breathless. Or was it that she was just ready and eager for love?

"You suddenly look sad," he said quietly. "Why?"

She was tempted to tell him. But, of course, she didn't. She hardly knew Lee Tyler.

"Will you produce the plays you're writing now?"

"I hope so. But who knows?"

Tish and Nollie appeared in the doorway.

"Listen, I offer to buy everyone a round of soda," Nollie said with a grin. "You two coming? We can go down to the drive-in."

"Let's go," Tish said. "It's a wonderful evening for a ride."

"We can go in my car," Lee said.

A few minutes later, they had climbed into Lee's old Chevrolet and with the windows down, the sea air blowing against their faces, they talked and laughed all the way down Beach Front Road to a drive-in, where car hops brought them frosted mugs of root beer.

"It's the simple pleasures in life that are the best," Nollie said, smacking his lips. "While I was hitchhiking here, I nearly died of thirst a few times."

Everyone laughed at that. By now, they all knew that Nollie was given to exaggeration. But it was a charming kind of flaw and no one really cared that it was there.

Tish told Nollie about her shop and he promised to drop in. Lee seemed quiet and thoughtful, his eyes hazy. Now and then he looked at Larina for a long moment until she looked away, cheeks warm. After a second round of root beer, Nollie said he wanted to go back to the playhouse and go for a walk on the beach.

"Will you join me, Tish?" he asked.

"Sure, if Lee and Larina will come along."

"Sounds like fun," Larina replied. "I love the beach even at night. It wouldn't be a bit hard for me to become a beachcomber."

Darkness had settled over Gull Haven when they went back. But the stars were bright in the warm, summer sky and now and then they heard a boat coming home and saw their running lights moving across the water.

Nollie skinned off his shoes and stockings and with a laugh, all of them followed suit. Lee reached a hand to Larina. His fingers closed around hers, warm and vibrant. Was it possible she felt a little tingle go along her arms?

With a laugh, Nollie snatched Tish's hand and began to run, pulling her along, Tish protesting loudly, her

blonde hair flying. Lee and Larina followed more
slowly.

"Have you been painting?" Lee asked.

"Yes. Quite a lot."

"Could I see sometime?"

"You should never ask an artist that!" she laughed.
"Don't you know that they'll trot out every line they
ever sketched?"

"Are you painting the sea?"

"Yes. The beach. Our dock. Our house. Everything."

The surf was rolling in, swishing its musical song. Lee
still grasped her hand and she had no desire to pull
away from his touch. He was comfortable to be with, his
voice was low and pleasant, and somehow they operated
on the same wavelength.

Ahead of them, Nollie had put an arm around Tish's
shoulders in a comradely way.

"They make a good pair," Lee said. "Both are so
outgoing. Sometimes, I wish I was more that way. Like
you—"

"Me?" Larina laughed.

"You're full of life. It spills out when you laugh and
the way your eyes light up. You believe everyone's good
and that the world is a wonderful place."

"Do I?" she asked.

"Don't you?"

"Yes, I suppose I do. Maybe I shouldn't be so—so—"

"Naïve?" Lee laughed. "No. Don't change, Larina. I
like you just as you are."

They had come near the Bleaker house. For a moment they stood and stared at it. The windows were
like empty eyes, seeing nothing. No life pulsed there.
Just empty rooms rubbing against other empty rooms.

"It's a dreary place," Lee frowned. "Why don't they do
something with it?"

"Oh, I don't know, I sort of like the old house. It's a
part of Gull Haven and this beach. As a little girl, I used
to be afraid of it. Now—well, I think it would make a
wonderful painting! Why didn't I think of that before?"

Lee laughed. "What will you call it?"

"I don't know. But I'll think of something," she answered. They walked on, leaving the Bleaker house behind. Nollie and Tish were ambling ahead of them, laughing and talking together as if they'd known each other all their lives.

With a sigh, Larina wondered where John was and what he was doing. Her father had promised to forward any mail that came. She hoped there would be an address where she could write him, although his plans had been to travel around the countryside, wherever his whim took him. Odd, she had expected him to write and she should have received a letter by now. Was he that busy? Or was he just no longer interested?

She brushed back a lock of hair from her forehead. She felt the sea air on her face and tried to think of the summer, of the plans she'd made, and she thought of Lee walking so quietly beside her, filled with his own thoughts. She could help at Calley's and she could be Jimmy's friend. But would it really erase this ache in her heart that came to her at odd moments such as these?

Nollie and Tish had stopped. They stood watching the sea.

"I'd like to sail with the tide," Nollie was saying. "I've only been abroad once. With a carnival. Wasn't the best time of my life, but I'd sure like to go back. To London I think. Perhaps France and Spain—"

"Talk to Nick, our gardener," Larina laughed. "He can fill your head full of all kinds of adventures and wanderlust."

"This guy's a nut," Tish said amusement. "An absolute nut!"

"Thanks," Nollie grinned. "I like you too, Tish. Say, you know, we make a pretty nice foursome. I hope we can all get together again sometime."

In the darkness, Larina knew that Lee was looking at her.

"Would you like that?" Lee asked.

"I—I'll see."

She knew they had all expected her to fall in with their plans. But she somehow felt tied to John. He had told her that she was to be free this summer. But somehow, it was a freedom she hadn't yet come to accept.

They turned back and walked toward the playhouse. Nollie and Tish loitered behind and soon Larina heard them singing together, loud and off key. They passed the Bleaker house again and Larina gave it one last glance. Perhaps tomorrow, she'd come here and set up her easel.

"What was that?" she asked with surprise.

"What?" Lee asked.

"I thought I saw a light inside there."

Lee stared at the house for a moment and shook his head.

"Maybe it was just a reflection from the street. Headlights shining in the windows or something."

"I—I thought—"

She broke off. It had to be her imagination.

"I know," she laughed. "We've been talking about them so much, we've stirred out the ghosts."

"Of course! That's it!" Lee agreed.

Linking arms, they left the beach and walked toward the theatre.

"Will you come in?" Lee asked.

"It's getting late. Tish has to open her store in the morning—"

"I'm not at all sure she cares about getting home," Lee said with amusement. "She and Nollie are still down on the beach. They seem to hit it off very well."

"Tish likes everyone."

"Do you?"

"Most generally," she admitted. "People can be a joy."

"Or a bore," he said wryly. "What about me, Larina? Do you like me?"

It was a very direct and unexpected question.

"You're a very nice person, Lee, and I wish you luck with the playhouse."

"I'm going to need it," he said. "That's why I'd like to have you on my side."

"All right," she nodded. "I'll do what I can to help. I'll paint backdrops like crazy!"

"Good! Thank you!"

Then to her surprise, he put his arms around her and drew her near. Before she could stop him, he had kissed her, warmly, gently, tenderly.

"Lee, I don't think I want to get involved with anyone this summer. Please, I hope you understand that."

"There's someone else?"

"Yes, I mean, I think there is—I mean—"

He laughed at that and touched her face with his long-fingered hand.

"Maybe I can change all of that, Larina. I'd like to try."

VIII

INSIDE THE BLEAKER HOUSE, a man dressed completely in black snapped off his flashlight. From the window, he had caught sight of some people on the beach.

"My luck," he muttered.

The last thing in the world he wanted to do was attract attention to the Bleaker house. Standing in the ruins of the old house, he smelled the dampness. The sea air had taken its toll and everywhere there was mildew, dust, cobwebs, and the chewing of mice.

He had been there for nearly an hour, watching and waiting. Taking his binoculars, he trained them once again on the water. Nothing. Once, he thought he might be in luck, but it turned out to be only a fishing boat, making a late run home. Staying near the windows, he had kneeled so that he was able to peer now and then over the high sill, but not be silhouetted. He spent most of the night there, back and knees aching, the stuffiness of the old house making it unpleasant to breathe. He drank from a thermos of cold water, munched a chocolate bar for energy and stared at the black water with its white rollers until it seemed he could see nothing at all.

"Dry run," he sighed. "Useless to stay any longer."

Something must have gone wrong. The signal should have come two nights ago and hadn't. He'd been here every night, waiting and watching.

"Tomorrow. Surely, they will come tomorrow."

Unless—no, he wouldn't think about that. It had to come off, without a hitch. There had been too much thought and planning put into the whole affair. It *had* to work! Pocketing the flashlight, patting his pocket to be sure his pistol was still there, he picked up the thermos, stood for a moment, thinking, making sure he was leaving nothing behind. He didn't want to risk the light again.

Slowly, carefully, he made his way through the enormous old house, went down the basement steps and hoisted himself out the small window that he had discovered was accessible because of a broken latch. Dusty, gulping in the fresh air, he ripped off the black gloves and eased himself into the shadows.

For a full ten minutes, he made himself stay there, watching, listening, making sure no one had been observing him. Then reassured, he shed the black shirt and trousers, stripping down to swimming trunks. Carefully he folded the clothes into a newspaper, tucked it under his arm and strode quickly to the beach. There, he walked along swiftly, breathing deeply, looking like a man with insomnia out for a walk along the water.

When he reached the house, he let himself in silently. He froze. Someone was there.

"Monroe?" he spoke quietly.

"Yeah. You're late."

"Wanted to be sure," he replied. "Absolutely sure."

"No show again tonight?" Monroe asked.

"No."

"Something's wrong. Something's gone screwy. Maybe they were tipped off."

"Maybe."

"Think we'd ought to check with the boss? Maybe change the plan?" Monroe asked.

"No! It *has* to go through. As planned."

"Yeah. Guess you're pretty anxious."

"Something like that."

"Listen, you want out?" Monroe asked. "If you do, say the word and the boss will fix it—"

"I don't want out," he replied evenly. "I thought I made that clear. I'm seeing it through to the delivery."

"A quarter million dollars!" Monroe whistled. "Makes your hair curl, doesn't it?"

"Where are they? What's keeping them?"

"Steady," Monroe said quietly. "Steady. We've been careful. Nobody's wise. I'm sure of it."

"I hope not. We can't goof, Monroe."

"I made some coffee. I think you could use it. You took the usual precautions, didn't you?"

"You don't have to tell me to do that, Monroe," he answered. "I'm not stupid. I'll never make that same mistake again—"

"Yeah. I guess you learned the hard way all right. Want the coffee now? Here or where?"

"The kitchen. You can go, Monroe. No need for you to stick around now. There's nothing brewing tonight and the sun will be up soon."

"Okay," Monroe said. "See you tomorrow."

"Usual time. You're getting sloppy about that, Monroe."

Monroe laughed quietly, coldly. "Sorry."

With a curt nod of his head, Monroe said good-bye and left. In a moment, the sound of a car starting quietly came to him. Pouring a cup of coffee, he carried it to a window and there, standing in the dark, he looked at the sea. The sky was growing lighter. Dawn would soon smudge it pink in the east, pushing the gray of the morning ahead of it, like a cover over a semicircle.

The ocean was so still, so empty.

"Where are they?" he muttered angrily. "Where are they?"

Larina didn't need an alarm clock to awaken at dawn. She had always been an early riser and the minute the sky began to grow light, she would open her eyes, stretch lazily, and swing her feet over the edge of the bed. Mornings in Gull Haven were special. At home, all she'd had to look forward to was a leisurely pot of coffee and time for a quick drawing or two in her sketch pad, or a review of the work she wanted her students to do in her art class at Riverdale High. Here, the entire beach waited for her.

Dressing in shorts and sneakers, and taking a plastic pail with her, she let herself out of the house quietly.

With a deep breath, she looked at the empty beach. At no other time of the day would it be so deserted.

Remembering Sutton Ward's promise to join her, she glanced toward his house. No light burned. He was probably sound asleep. Still, he had promised—

With a mischievous laugh, she decided to pay him a visit, roust him out. She half walked, half ran across the sand to the Bardwell house. Crossing the patio, she knocked at the glass doors. Peering inside, she couldn't see anyone stirring.

"Hey, Sutton! Sutton!"

She rattled the doors loudly, but either he was a sound sleeper or he wasn't there. Giving up at last, she turned away. She did hope the poor man wasn't ill. After her experience with him yesterday, it rather worried her.

Humming, greeting the sun with a smile, she went down to the water's edge. From somewhere, a small dog came bounding toward her, yipping and wagging his tail.

"Well, hello, pooch," Larina said. She bent down and rubbed his ears. In reply to her friendliness, he danced around her. Then as she proceeded on down the beach, he fell in step beside her. With every shell she retrieved, he was there, poking his nose against it, examining it.

"Okay, pooch? Shall I keep this one?"

They went on, a small young woman and a tiny dog, talking to each other, finding freshly washed shells, prodding out still others from the sand with a large broken conch.

After nearly an hour, she turned and went back toward Sea Mist. Returning to the house, she looked toward Sutton's place. But there was still no sign of life.

Aunt Stell was also an early riser and she was in the dining room in a fancy negligee, having her first cup of coffee.

"Good morning, Aunt Stell!"

"Hello, dear. Have any luck?"

"Not much. Maybe I'm getting too selective. How are you? How's your wrist?"

"Bothersome. But it will soon be as good as new. We

had an interesting meeting last night. Naturally most of it concerned the problem at Calley's."

"Still no new ideas?"

"No. The club is determined to raise money. But heaven knows how we'll ever manage to get all we need. The place needs so much work done: painting, new plumbing, goodness knows what all."

"I've tried to think of something unique, Aunt Stell, and I've come up blank! But I'll do my best."

Aunt Stell smiled. "I wish all our members had your enthusiasm."

"You enjoy your club work, don't you?"

Aunt Stell sighed heavily. "Yes. To a point. I hate being idle and with your uncle away—well, the days do get long. I wish Bert—"

"No word from him?"

"The last we knew, he was in Istanbul. What he was doing there, I haven't the vaguest idea! He dropped us a very short note saying he was going to Mexico next. Since that's just across the Gulf, I was hoping he'd spend some time here this summer."

"Maybe he will. I wish he would!" Larina said enthusiastically. "Bert and I always have so much fun together."

"Bert's been a disappointment to his father. Not that Ernie doesn't love him, he does. But Bert couldn't care less about being a banker and Ernie had hoped—"

"Bert will never be any more than what he is. A very carefree, country-hopping young man in search of fun, excitement, new faces, and new places."

"That's Bert. Sometimes, I think my sister was wrong to leave him all that money. But he is a grown man. We can't make him stay here."

"Bert will be home. Wait and see. He likes to fly from country to country, like a bee buzzing around the flowers, but he always comes home eventually—doesn't he? Like a bee to the hive?"

"That's an odd comparison," Aunt Stell smiled. "But, yes, you're right, Larina. He always comes home."

"I hope he comes while I'm here," Larina said wistfully.

told her that she was to be free this summer. But somehow, it was a freedom she hadn't yet come to accept.

They turned back and walked toward the playhouse. Nollie and Tish loitered behind and soon Larina heard them singing together, loud and off key. They passed the Bleaker house again and Larina gave it one last glance. Perhaps tomorrow, she'd come here and set up her easel.

"What was that?" she asked with surprise.

"What?" Lee asked.

"I thought I saw a light inside there."

Lee stared at the house for a moment and shook his head.

"Maybe it was just a reflection from the street. Headlights shining in the windows or something."

"I—I thought—"

She broke off. It had to be her imagination.

"I know," she laughed. "We've been talking about them so much, we've stirred out the ghosts."

"Of course! That's it!" Lee agreed.

Linking arms, they left the beach and walked toward the theatre.

"Will you come in?" Lee asked.

"It's getting late. Tish has to open her store in the morning—"

"I'm not at all sure she cares about getting home," Lee said with amusement. "She and Nollie are still down on the beach. They seem to hit it off very well."

"Tish likes everyone."

"Do you?"

"Most generally," she admitted. "People can be a joy."

"Or a bore," he said wryly. "What about me, Larina? Do you like me?"

It was a very direct and unexpected question.

"You're a very nice person, Lee, and I wish you luck with the playhouse."

"I'm going to need it," he said. "That's why I'd like to have you on my side."

"All right," she nodded. "I'll do what I can to help. I'll paint backdrops like crazy!"

"Good! Thank you!"

swered. They walked on, leaving the Bleaker house behind. Nollie and Tish were ambling ahead of them, laughing and talking together as if they'd known each other all their lives.

With a sigh, Larina wondered where John was and what he was doing. Her father had promised to forward any mail that came. She hoped there would be an address where she could write him, although his plans had been to travel around the countryside, wherever his whim took him. Odd, she had expected him to write and she should have received a letter by now. Was he that busy? Or was he just no longer interested?

She brushed back a lock of hair from her forehead. She felt the sea air on her face and tried to think of the summer, of the plans she'd made, and she thought of Lee walking so quietly beside her, filled with his own thoughts. She could help at Calley's and she could be Jimmy's friend. But would it really erase this ache in her heart that came to her at odd moments such as these?

Nollie and Tish had stopped. They stood watching the sea.

"I'd like to sail with the tide," Nollie was saying. "I've only been abroad once. With a carnival. Wasn't the best time of my life, but I'd sure like to go back. To London I think. Perhaps France and Spain—"

"Talk to Nick, our gardener," Larina laughed. "He can fill your head full of all kinds of adventures and wanderlust."

"This guy's a nut," Tish said amusement. "An absolute nut!"

"Thanks," Nollie grinned. "I like you too, Tish. Say, you know, we make a pretty nice foursome. I hope we can all get together again sometime."

In the darkness, Larina knew that Lee was looking at her.

"Would you like that?" Lee asked.

"I—I'll see."

She knew they had all expected her to fall in with their plans. But she somehow felt tied to John. He had

Lee took a deep breath. "Anywhere you want, so long as you stay out of my hair."

"Gotcha!" Nollie laughed. "Hey, this is great! Beautiful weather down here. Never been here in the summer time. Played here once in the winter. Rained the whole time. But this is great. Listen, I think I'll take a dip in the surf. Want to come along?"

Lee started to shake his head. Then on second thought, changed his mind.

"All right, Nollie. I believe I will."

He found Nollie on the beach fifteen minutes later, a skinny, redheaded guy almost going berserk, running pell-mell into the surf. There, he splashed and shouted and cavorted like a small boy. His enthusiasm was contagious. Lee couldn't remember enjoying the Gulf as much as he did that afternoon.

Splashing out at last, they spread beach towels and basked in the sun. Nollie was a name-dropper. His tales and talk ran from the unforgettable Helen Hayes to Barbra Streisand, from Olivier to Mick Jagger.

"Nollie, how did you hear about the playhouse?" Lee asked.

Nollie rested his head on his hand, elbow bent and dug into the sand. "Believe it or not," he shrugged. "I read it in a paper in New York. Just a little item in one of the show-business columns. Somebody must have heard about it, printed it, and here I am!"

Lee frowned. Odd. Gull Haven was not well known and certainly no one in New York could be interested in the old playhouse. But then he supposed some writer was hungry for material and had used whatever he could find.

"Hey, want to hear me do Shakespeare?" Nollie asked. "*King Lear?*"

Lee grinned. This guy was a nut! But refreshing too. Just the sort of general, all-around know-it-all that they could use this summer.

"Okay, *King Lear*. Go!"

Nollie began spouting Shakespeare and Lee had resigned himself to being bored. But surprisingly, Nollie

spoke with a great deal of eloquence and dramatic effect. Lee became absorbed.

When Nollie had finished his scene at last, Lee stared at him.

"You're for real!"

"Didn't you think I would be?" Nollie asked. "Just never got the breaks, man. That's all."

"I believe we'll be able to use you, Nollie."

"I'll earn my keep. That's a promise," Nollie said. "Say, you know, things are beginning to look up for Hans Oliver. Yes sir, they surely are."

Nollie went from Shakespeare to Arthur Miller to William Inge to Thornton Wilder's *Our Town*.

When he broke off at last, there was a frown on his face and his gaze was directed down the beach.

"Who's that?"

Lee glanced over his shoulder. The man was tall, had black hair, wore sunglasses and walked in a stiff-legged sort of way.

"Lives around here I think," Lee replied. "Down the beach. I see him walking along here often."

"Yeah?" Nollie asked. "What's his name?"

Lee shook his head. "I don't know. Never met the man. I haven't been here very long myself."

"Funny. Looks familiar somehow. Wonder where I met him?"

"Who can say about that?" Lee asked lightly. "You've been everywhere, done everything, met so many important people—"

"You're right," Nollie grinned. "Just my imagination."

The man had spotted them. He paused, bent to pick up a shell, gazed out to the horizon for a moment, and then turned back. Funny. He always walked on past the theatre, and followed the beach to the old dock before turning back.

"Friendly cuss, isn't he?" Nollie asked.

"Believe it or not, Nollie, there are a few people who don't run off the head to everyone they meet."

"Meaning I do?" Nollie asked with a grin. "Sorry. It's just me bloomin' personality."

Lee got up to brush the sand from his trunks. The

afternoon was getting away and the typewriter still waited. There was a knotty scene in his play that was very vital and giving him great difficulty. He couldn't solve it by lolling about the beach.

"Listen, anything you want me to do?" Nollie asked.

"Sure," Lee said. "Give me a few hours' peace and quiet. If you want to work, those prop rooms need to be straightened and cleaned. See what you can find that's salvageable that we can use this summer."

"Sure thing, Lee. I'll get right with it. Soon as I take another snooze. Man, this air gets to you."

Lee nodded and walked away. Reaching the old inn, he glanced back. Nollie wasn't sleeping on the sand. He was up and walking away, following the man in the sunglasses at a discreet distance. What did it matter to a man like Nollie who the stranger was or where he lived or what he did or why he had so pointedly avoided them?

Then with a shrug, Lee decided it was none of his business and went inside.

VI

FOR THE NEXT FEW DAYS, Larina painted for long, dedicated sessions, trying very hard to lose herself in her work. Occasionally she took her easel to the beach, but most of the time she used her new studio. She hadn't seen Sutton Ward again. Perhaps he was away for a few days.

When she felt herself going stale, she covered her easel and told Aunt Stella that she wanted to visit Calley's Home for Children.

"But your work—"

"I need a break!" Larina told her. "Besides, you've talked so much about little Jimmy Baker that I'm dying to see him!"

"We'll go over this morning," Aunt Stella promised.

The Home was about twenty minutes away from Beach Front Road. Driving there, Larina remembered the last time she had visited. She had come to know most of the children there. Of course, some of them would be gone now. It had been over a year since she'd last been here. But there were always a few that got left, who never found adoptive parents or even a foster home.

"We're looking for a novel idea to raise money," Aunt Stella sighed. "If you can think of anything—pass it along!"

The Home seemed shabbier than ever. Even Larina's inexperienced eyes saw that the place badly needed repairs. The children were outside, playing, and when they saw the convertible, they stopped to stare. But Aunt Stella was a familiar sight there and they knew she

44

was not a prospective parent, so they went back to their noisy games.

"Over there," Aunt Stella said. "By himself. He's still a little withdrawn. Doesn't join the others very much. Come along, Larina. I'll introduce you."

Jimmy Baker was about six, with brown hair, large brown eyes that could melt Larina with just one look, a dirt smudged, pale little face and expressive hands. His shoulders were rigid and his eyes suspicious.

"Hello, Jimmy," Aunt Stella said. "I've brought you a new friend. This is Larina."

"Hello, Jimmy," Larina said.

"I'll leave you two while I go inside," Aunt Stell said.

Jimmy was leaning against an old pine tree, hands stuffed into his pockets.

"Don't you like to play games, Jimmy?"

"No!" he said crossly.

"Oh. Well, in that case, let's go for a walk."

"No."

"Please? With sugar and cream?" Larina asked.

She gave him a smile and he stared at her for a moment with huge, brown eyes.

"No."

Larina shrugged her shoulders. "Okay. I didn't really want to go anyway."

He was watching her carefully. Larina picked up a stick and began scratching in the sand, making a picture of a round faced boy with a sad mouth.

"Sad Jimmy," Larina sighed. "That's what we'll call him."

He was getting curious. After a moment, he edged a little closer for a better look.

"Shall we change him?" Larina asked.

Jimmy didn't answer. She paid no attention, but drew another face in the sand and this time, added a big smile.

"Oh, that does something for him, doesn't it?" Larina asked.

Jimmy stared at the sand drawing, keeping his hands in his pockets.

"I draw pictures. Lots of pictures. Someday, maybe I'll make a painting of you. Wouldn't that be fun?"

"Maybe."

She laughed and gave her dark head a toss. Then reaching into her pocket, she held out a closed fist toward him.

"Present. Go on, take it."

He held back. She wiggled her fist. "It won't bite," she promised.

Finally, he extended his hand and she dropped the gift into his small palm.

"It's a seashell," she said. "I found it on our beach. Isn't it pretty?"

He fingered it, turning it over and over, examining it from all angles.

"The next time I come, I'll bring you a great big one. You can hold it up to your ear and hear the sea in it!"

"Oh."

She laughed again and reached out a hand. For a moment, he seemed to shrink back.

"Oh, Jimmy, I just want to be a friend. Okay?"

"Never had a friend."

"Well! You have now!"

This time, he allowed her to touch him. She grasped his shoulders in her hands and tugged him closer. She could see the golden specks in his brown eyes and the texture of his thick hair.

"Do you like dogs?" she asked.

He nodded his head.

"I saw a nice little pooch on our beach the other day. Maybe if you come and visit sometime, you could play with him."

"When?"

She laughed and ruffled his hair. "Well, soon. I promise. It will be soon."

During the short time she was there, she urged him to take part in some of the games the other children were playing. He would do it only when she joined them herself. So for a vigorous thirty minutes or so, while Aunt Stell was busy inside, she played tag, hide and seek, and London Bridge is falling down.

Then at last, it was time to go. Jimmy followed her to the car.

"Good-bye, Jimmy," Larina said. "I'll see you soon."

"When's soon?" he asked.

She brushed back his hair from his forehead and looked into the brown eyes. Her soul was lost in that moment and she knew it. Her trouble was that she couldn't resist children like this. She was always too softhearted about everything.

"Not tomorrow. But maybe the next day. Whenever I can, I'll come. Okay?"

He nodded vigorously.

"Still have your shell?" she asked.

He dug eagerly into his pocket and found it, holding it up for her to see.

"Keep it," she said. "It will be like a promise in your pocket." Then she gave him a brief hug and climbed into the car. He waved and was still watching them as she looked back for one last time.

"How do you do it, Larina?" Aunt Stell asked.

"Do what?"

"Melt down little boys like that? Do you know he's been very withdrawn ever since he came. Yet, just a few minutes with you—"

Larina was secretly pleased. She laughed and blinked back tears at the same time.

"Oh, I don't know. We just communicated some way. I think kids sense things. He knew I liked him on sight."

"Ah, Larina!" Aunt Stell laughed. "You're so quick to love!"

"Who couldn't love a little boy like that?" Larina wondered.

Aunt Stell frowned.

"I suppose his mother *did* love him. I don't know."

The effect of being with Jimmy stayed with Larina for a long time. It was never completely gone, but lingered in the corners of her heart. Sometimes, working at her easel, she would pause and look out to the sea, thinking about Jimmy. Somehow, it brought the problem of drugs and their users closer to home.

After a particularly busy and tiring day at the easel,

she decided to go for a swim in the Gulf. The beach was sloping and the tides were predictable in this area. Even though there was no danger swimming here, it always seemed to be a challenge to Larina. It was fun to pit her strength against the oncoming waves, to swim away from the shore into the infinitive expanse of blue water.

She swam for nearly half an hour until she began to feel tired and relaxed. Splashing out, she spread a beach towel and stretched out to dry in the sun.

The sun made her drowsy and she must have dozed, for when she opened her eyes, the sun was blotted out and she realized someone was standing over her, between her and the sun. For a moment, she blinked.

"Hello."

Sutton Ward!

"You know the story about the proverbial bad penny," he said in his low, pleasant voice. "Here I am again. I thought of waking you but you seemed so peaceful."

"I was," she laughed. "I was drifting with the tide."

He smiled at that. Then without invitation, he sat down beside her on the sand, stretching out his long, brown legs. She had never seen him in anything but swimming trunks and she wondered in a curious way how he would look in a suit and tie.

"Tell me, Larina, are you interested in the summer theatre they're opening up this summer?"

"I'm a little curious," she said. "Why? Are you?"

"I've walked up there a few times. Activity seems to be picking up. It must be fun. I've—I've never had the opportunity to join anything like that. Do you suppose they could use a man like me?"

This surprised her. Sutton Ward hardly seemed the type.

"What talents do you have? Would you be another Barrymore?" she teased.

He laughed and his white teeth flashed. She wished he weren't so good looking.

"As I told you before, Larina, I have no talent. But perhaps there would be something I could do."

"You hardly seem the sort—"

"I enjoy life, Larina. I like poking my nose into new

things. Frankly, I've been a little bored here. After the first few days of soaking in the sun, I began to get restless."

"Does that mean you'll be off to Monte Carlo or some other exotic place?"

He shook his head quickly. "No. I'll spend the summer here, as I planned. Do you know anyone connected with the playhouse?"

"Yes. I'll pass the word on if you like. I'm sure they'll contact you."

"I'd be most grateful," he said. "Thank you."

He pulled his legs up and wrapped his arms around them. The sun made his black hair seem glossy and his eyelashes were thick and long. But probably his most fascinating feature were his gray eyes. Cool one moment, hot the next. There was a shrewd intelligence to the man.

The surf came crashing in and she watched the rollers breaking, making the *Mary Belle* rock where it was moored at the dock.

"We're going to get caught in the next few minutes," he laughed. "The tide's coming in."

"I should be getting back anyway," she answered.

She got to her feet and he leaped up at the same time. Then with a gasp, he put both hands to the small of his back and bit down hard on his lip. His face was contorted with pain. His gray eyes were abruptly dull, all light gone out of them.

"What is it?" she asked with alarm. "What's wrong, Sutton?"

"Sorry," he muttered. "I—I have these spasms occasionally. I—I hate to ask, but would you help me home?"

She nodded. "Of course. Oh, dear, is it bad?"

"If you'd just let me lean on you, I think I can manage it."

His arm draped heavily around her shoulders and he began walking, partially stooped, his face white and breaking out with perspiration.

"Should I call for help?" she asked.

"No. No. Please. I'd rather you didn't. I'm a little

sensitive about this. I—I suppose no man likes to have trouble navigating on his own. I'm sorry it had to happen in front of you—"

"Don't talk," she said. "Just concentrate on getting to the house."

His steps were labored and his weight was becoming unbearable. The poor man! She wished there was more she could do!

"Serves me right," he muttered. "I should never leave the house without my capsules."

They were nearing the Bardwell house at last. He looked with anxious longing at the chaise longue on the patio. With one final effort, he stepped up to the stone floor and with care, she helped him ease down to the chaise.

"Lie back," she said. "Rest. You're exhausted."

"My capsules—they will help immensely."

"I'll get them for you, if you'll tell me where they are."

"My bedroom. On the bedside table. First door to the right off the hall. Please, hurry—"

She fled into the strange house. She had never been inside the Bardwell house before. She found it to be very luxurious, tastefully furnished, and spotlessly clean. It was almost as if no one lived here. It took a few moments, but she located the bedroom. The bottle of capsules weren't where he said they would be.

Glancing about, she spied a jacket hanging on the back of a chair. He was probably in the habit of carrying them with him. Without a moment's hesitation, she thrust her hand into the pockets. There was something hard and heavy in the inner breast pocket. She felt it swinging there as she tried first one side pocket and then another.

"There!" she said triumphantly.

The vial was half filled with white capsules. Rushing back to the patio, she went to bend over him. He was lying very still, with his eyes closed. She put a cool hand to his forehead.

"Sutton—"

He stirred. "Thank you. You found them. There's a pitcher of water over there on the table."

Then with a nod, he turned away. She stepped down into the white sand. She had just been given the bum's rush and it had surprised her. Sutton had been so warm and charming only a moment ago! Glancing back, she saw him walking swiftly toward the door. For the first time, she noticed the little white scars just above the band of his swimming trunks. He said he'd undergone surgery. Yet, the scars didn't look like an incision a surgeon would make.

Puzzled, intrigued, and more than just a little curious, she walked through the sand toward Sea Mist.

"Yoo-hoo, Larina!"

Someone was calling to her. With a wave of her arm, she saw Tish Morgan waiting for her.

"What were you doing over there?" Tish wondered with a curious expression on her pretty face.

"You'd never believe it!" she said.

"Sutton Ward lives there, doesn't he?"

"Do you know Sutton?" Larina asked with surprise.

"He's been in my shop a time or two. Handsome devil, isn't he?"

"Yes," Larina admitted. "What do you know about him, Tish?"

"Not much. Listen, I'm on my way to the playhouse. Why don't you come along."

"Why not?" Larina said.

VII

A SHORT TIME LATER, Larina, dressed in a green dress of a soft, cool material, joined Tish.

"So, all right, when do you tell me?" Tish wondered as they drove away from Sea Mist.

"Tell you what?"

"What you were doing at Sutton Ward's house!" Tish said with exasperation. "Honestly, don't you know he's just about the most eligible new man in Gull Haven? There are several women I know who would give their eye teeth to get inside his door!"

Larina laughed. "Oh, really, Tish. He's just an ordinary man. A little lonely and a terrible cook. I fixed some steak. He ate as if he was starving!"

"Larina Goodwin, you amaze me. You sound as if that's something you do every day!"

"Well, I usually cook for Dad."

Tish shook her blonde hair and turned her attention to her driving. It didn't take long to reach the far end of the beach. Soon, they were going past the Bleaker house.

"Such a shame about that place," Larina said. "I imagine it was once a very lovely home."

"Yes. I never could understand why they just let it stand. No one lives there. Can't they rent it or sell it?"

Larina shook her head. "As I understand there's some kind of legal snarl that's been dragging on for years. Meanwhile, the house just sits there and grows older."

"Sort of spooky, isn't it? A perfect setting for ghosts."

"If you believed in them."

"Knowing you, I'm surprised you don't!" Tish teased.

Whisking past the Bleaker house, they soon saw the old inn that had been made over into a summer theatre. Tish brought the car to a bouncing halt.

"Sounds like some activity inside," Tish said.

"Either that or they're tearing the place down!'"

The old inn had once been a popular place in Gull Haven, although it was before Larina's time. Uncle Ernie had told her about it. Now, the place could seat about a hundred and fifty people. The stage was not large, but adequate. A red-haired, wiry man was busy working on some old props, wielding a hammer with a savage determination.

"Hi," Tish called. "Where's Lee?"

"In his office," came the reply.

Lee heard their voices and came out. There was a harried look on his face as he put a pencil behind his ear.

"Well, hello," he said.

"How's things going, Lee?" Tish asked.

"Slow. Much too slow. If we're not careful the summer will get away and we won't have nearly enough plays produced." -

"We go into rehearsal next week, don't we?"

"Yes. If we can just get the sets ready and the props gathered up."

"New volunteer?" Tish asked nodding toward the red-haired man.

Lee smiled. Larina noticed how it lighted up his hazel eyes.

"Come along. I'll introduce you."

It was Hans Oliver, who immediately explained that everyone called him Nollie. Nollie and Tish seemed to get along especially well.

"Could I show you around, Larina?" Lee asked.

Larina nodded. "I'd love to see it. I've been here but I'd forgotten what it really looked like. Do you expect a good season?"

Lee grinned again. "We always hope, don't we?"

He took her into every room at the theatre and she saw all the dusty old props and the backdrops with their faded paint.

"You can see why we need your services, Larina," he explained. "We'll be starting to work on these in the next day or so. The plan is to rehearse a couple of hours every evening and then spend the rest of the time working on the sets."

"What do you need?"

Lee's eyes flickered. "You mean, you'll help us?"

"I'll do what I can. It looks like fun. I've never been involved with anything like this."

"First we'll need a country scene. All of the first act takes place there. Then an interior setting. I think we've got enough decent stuff to use for that. The last act calls for a railroad depot."

"I see."

Lee took her arm and guided her into the last room which at one time had been an office. Now she saw that he had fixed it up as living quarters. The desk was filled with sheets of paper and the typewriter stood there waiting like some dark animal about to pounce.

"You've been working. We shouldn't have interrupted."

"I let Nollie talk me into going for a swim this afternoon so I got behind," he replied. "But I was more than ready for a break."

"What's the name of your play?"

"*The Way of Love.*"

"Sounds interesting," she said with a teasing smile. "Writing from experience?"

His hazel eyes met hers. Then he gave her a quick shake of his head. "No. Not really. There's never been a girl I was really in love with. Oh, there were a few school crushes, you know the bit—"

She thought of John. There had been nice boys in high school. Nicer ones in college. But there had never really been anyone in her life until John Adair. He had come on with a rush that left her breathless. Or was it that she was just ready and eager for love?

"You suddenly look sad," he said quietly. "Why?"

She was tempted to tell him. But, of course, she didn't. She hardly knew Lee Tyler.

"Will you produce the plays you're writing now?"

"I hope so. But who knows?"

Tish and Nollie appeared in the doorway.

"Listen, I offer to buy everyone a round of soda," Nollie said with a grin. "You two coming? We can go down to the drive-in."

"Let's go," Tish said. "It's a wonderful evening for a ride."

"We can go in my car," Lee said.

A few minutes later, they had climbed into Lee's old Chevrolet and with the windows down, the sea air blowing against their faces, they talked and laughed all the way down Beach Front Road to a drive-in, where car hops brought them frosted mugs of root beer.

"It's the simple pleasures in life that are the best," Nollie said, smacking his lips. "While I was hitchhiking here, I nearly died of thirst a few times."

Everyone laughed at that. By now, they all knew that Nollie was given to exaggeration. But it was a charming kind of flaw and no one really cared that it was there.

Tish told Nollie about her shop and he promised to drop in. Lee seemed quiet and thoughtful, his eyes hazy. Now and then he looked at Larina for a long moment until she looked away, cheeks warm. After a second round of root beer, Nollie said he wanted to go back to the playhouse and go for a walk on the beach.

"Will you join me, Tish?" he asked.

"Sure, if Lee and Larina will come along."

"Sounds like fun," Larina replied. "I love the beach even at night. It wouldn't be a bit hard for me to become a beachcomber."

Darkness had settled over Gull Haven when they went back. But the stars were bright in the warm, summer sky and now and then they heard a boat coming home and saw their running lights moving across the water.

Nollie skinned off his shoes and stockings and with a laugh, all of them followed suit. Lee reached a hand to Larina. His fingers closed around hers, warm and vibrant. Was it possible she felt a little tingle go along her arms?

With a laugh, Nollie snatched Tish's hand and began to run, pulling her along, Tish protesting loudly, her

blonde hair flying. Lee and Larina followed more slowly.

"Have you been painting?" Lee asked.

"Yes. Quite a lot."

"Could I see sometime?"

"You should never ask an artist that!" she laughed. "Don't you know that they'll trot out every line they ever sketched?"

"Are you painting the sea?"

"Yes. The beach. Our dock. Our house. Everything."

The surf was rolling in, swishing its musical song. Lee still grasped her hand and she had no desire to pull away from his touch. He was comfortable to be with, his voice was low and pleasant, and somehow they operated on the same wavelength.

Ahead of them, Nollie had put an arm around Tish's shoulders in a comradely way.

"They make a good pair," Lee said. "Both are so outgoing. Sometimes, I wish I was more that way. Like you—"

"Me?" Larina laughed.

"You're full of life. It spills out when you laugh and the way your eyes light up. You believe everyone's good and that the world is a wonderful place."

"Do I?" she asked.

"Don't you?"

"Yes, I suppose I do. Maybe I shouldn't be so—so—"

"Naïve?" Lee laughed. "No. Don't change, Larina. I like you just as you are."

They had come near the Bleaker house. For a moment they stood and stared at it. The windows were like empty eyes, seeing nothing. No life pulsed there. Just empty rooms rubbing against other empty rooms.

"It's a dreary place," Lee frowned. "Why don't they do something with it?"

"Oh, I don't know, I sort of like the old house. It's a part of Gull Haven and this beach. As a little girl, I used to be afraid of it. Now—well, I think it would make a wonderful painting! Why didn't I think of that before?"

Lee laughed. "What will you call it?"

"I don't know. But I'll think of something," she an-

sure his pistol was still there, he picked up the thermos, stood for a moment, thinking, making sure he was leaving nothing behind. He didn't want to risk the light again.

Slowly, carefully, he made his way through the enormous old house, went down the basement steps and hoisted himself out the small window that he had discovered was accessible because of a broken latch. Dusty, gulping in the fresh air, he ripped off the black gloves and eased himself into the shadows.

For a full ten minutes, he made himself stay there, watching, listening, making sure no one had been observing him. Then reassured, he shed the black shirt and trousers, stripping down to swimming trunks. Carefully he folded the clothes into a newspaper, tucked it under his arm and strode quickly to the beach. There, he walked along swiftly, breathing deeply, looking like a man with insomnia out for a walk along the water.

When he reached the house, he let himself in silently. He froze. Someone was there.

"Monroe?" he spoke quietly.

"Yeah. You're late."

"Wanted to be sure," he replied. "Absolutely sure."

"No show again tonight?" Monroe asked.

"No."

"Something's wrong. Something's gone screwy. Maybe they were tipped off."

"Maybe."

"Think we'd ought to check with the boss? Maybe change the plan?" Monroe asked.

"No! It *has* to go through. As planned."

"Yeah. Guess you're pretty anxious."

"Something like that."

"Listen, you want out?" Monroe asked. "If you do, say the word and the boss will fix it—"

"I don't want out," he replied evenly. "I thought I made that clear. I'm seeing it through to the delivery."

"A quarter million dollars!" Monroe whistled. "Makes your hair curl, doesn't it?"

"Where are they? What's keeping them?"

"Steady," Monroe said quietly. "Steady. We've been careful. Nobody's wise. I'm sure of it."

"I hope not. We can't goof, Monroe."

"I made some coffee. I think you could use it. You took the usual precautions, didn't you?"

"You don't have to tell me to do that, Monroe," he answered. "I'm not stupid. I'll never make that same mistake again—"

"Yeah. I guess you learned the hard way all right. Want the coffee now? Here or where?"

"The kitchen. You can go, Monroe. No need for you to stick around now. There's nothing brewing tonight and the sun will be up soon."

"Okay," Monroe said. "See you tomorrow."

"Usual time. You're getting sloppy about that, Monroe."

Monroe laughed quietly, coldly. "Sorry."

With a curt nod of his head, Monroe said good-bye and left. In a moment, the sound of a car starting quietly came to him. Pouring a cup of coffee, he carried it to a window and there, standing in the dark, he looked at the sea. The sky was growing lighter. Dawn would soon smudge it pink in the east, pushing the gray of the morning ahead of it, like a cover over a semicircle.

The ocean was so still, so empty.

"Where are they?" he muttered angrily. "Where are they?"

Larina didn't need an alarm clock to awaken at dawn. She had always been an early riser and the minute the sky began to grow light, she would open her eyes, stretch lazily, and swing her feet over the edge of the bed. Mornings in Gull Haven were special. At home, all she'd had to look forward to was a leisurely pot of coffee and time for a quick drawing or two in her sketch pad, or a review of the work she wanted her students to do in her art class at Riverdale High. Here, the entire beach waited for her.

Dressing in shorts and sneakers, and taking a plastic pail with her, she let herself out of the house quietly.

Then to her surprise, he put his arms around her and drew her near. Before she could stop him, he had kissed her, warmly, gently, tenderly.

"Lee, I don't think I want to get involved with anyone this summer. Please, I hope you understand that."

"There's someone else?"

"Yes, I mean, I think there is—I mean—"

He laughed at that and touched her face with his long-fingered hand.

"Maybe I can change all of that, Larina. I'd like to try."

VIII

Inside the Bleaker house, a man dressed completely in black snapped off his flashlight. From the window, he had caught sight of some people on the beach.

"My luck," he muttered.

The last thing in the world he wanted to do was attract attention to the Bleaker house. Standing in the ruins of the old house, he smelled the dampness. The sea air had taken its toll and everywhere there was mildew, dust, cobwebs, and the chewing of mice.

He had been there for nearly an hour, watching and waiting. Taking his binoculars, he trained them once again on the water. Nothing. Once, he thought he might be in luck, but it turned out to be only a fishing boat, making a late run home. Staying near the windows, he had kneeled so that he was able to peer now and then over the high sill, but not be silhouetted. He spent most of the night there, back and knees aching, the stuffiness of the old house making it unpleasant to breathe. He drank from a thermos of cold water, munched a chocolate bar for energy and stared at the black water with its white rollers until it seemed he could see nothing at all.

"Dry run," he sighed. "Useless to stay any longer."

Something must have gone wrong. The signal should have come two nights ago and hadn't. He'd been here every night, waiting and watching.

"Tomorrow. Surely, they will come tomorrow."

Unless—no, he wouldn't think about that. It had to come off, without a hitch. There had been too much thought and planning put into the whole affair. It *had* to work! Pocketing the flashlight, patting his pocket to be

She filled a glass and brought it back to him. While she watched, he swallowed two of the capsules.

"Are you going to be all right?" she asked anxiously.

"Yes. In a few minutes. Larina, I'm sorry to be such a bother."

"It's all right, but you gave me a fright! Do you often have these spasms?"

"Yes. But I've been told they will pass. I—I had some surgery a few months ago. I suppose I might as well tell you. That's really why I came to Gull Haven. It's a quiet place and I needed rest badly. Give myself time to heal."

"I see. What a shame! But if any place can help surely it's Gull Haven."

"Most of the time, I'm quite well. But having a tricky back can be a problem," he admitted.

She sat down opposite him. Somehow, seeing him like this, he no longer seemed so arrogant and cocksure. In a way, she liked him more for it.

"Funny," he murmured. "I had hoped to impress you, to perhaps have you as a guest in my house. Now, you're here—and I'm flat on my back and being a nuisance."

She laughed. "It's quite all right, Sutton. You do have a lovely house. Are you here alone?"

"Yes. I have a woman that comes in twice a week to clean, do the laundry, and things like that."

"It's a big house for one man."

"I'll grant you that. But I never liked being cooped up, Larina. Always needed space."

"Are you feeling better now? Could I get you anything else?"

He shook his head and gingerly sat up. Running a hand over his black hair, he gave her a careful smile.

"No. The capsules are working. They're fast. I'm glad of that."

"Do you think it's wise to be here alone?"

He looked at her for a long moment. "Yes. It's all right. Perhaps I overdid the swimming this afternoon. The Gulf waters were recommended to me and they have relieved the soreness tremendously. But I do limit my-

self to a few minutes at a time. Gradually, I'll work up to longer periods in the water."

"It's like therapy?"

"Yes, that's a good word for it, Larina. So, I've become sort of a beach bum. The sun has restored my energy too."

He seemed to be getting over his painful seizure and when he said there was nothing more for her to do, she said she should be getting back.

"I wish you'd stay. Keep me company."

"It's getting late. Bertha will be expecting me for dinner. Aunt Stell's going to be away and I told Bertha I'd eat early tonight. That way, she can have the evening free—"

Sutton smiled at her. "You're a very thoughtful girl. In fact, why don't you stay here?" he asked again. "Say, can you cook?"

She laughed. "Of course I can cook! I always cooked at home and especially after Mother died."

"I can't. I'm horrible in the kitchen. Sometimes I phone and have my meals delivered. I can manage some pretty bad coffee, but not much else."

She began to see what he really wanted. She was amused and surprised. But why not? The poor man was ill. Like so many men, he was helpless when it came to preparing food.

"You want me to stay and make dinner?"

"Would you?" he asked hopefully. "For the two of us."

"I'd like to help, but—"

"Good! Then you'll stay."

Sutton seemed so eager. Like a hungry, lost boy in need of help.

"All right," she laughed. "What would you like?"

"Anything. Just anything. If you can't find it in the kitchen, I'll get it," he said, his face lighting up.

"You might be sorry," she told him. "I'm not a gourmet chef."

There was one pause on the way to the kitchen to phone Bertha that she would not be there after all. The kitchen was modern in every way. Inside the huge refrigerator, she found ample supplies. With Sutton

perched on a step stool, she tied a dish towel around her waist and went to work. Soon the fragrance of broiling steak filled the air. Sutton leaned against the counter, watching with his gray eyes. His color had returned and he was able to walk upright again.

"Steak is my father's favorite," she said.

"Your father? Where is he?"

"Home in Riverdale. An attorney. I feel a little guilty coming here for the summer and leaving him alone."

"But we do have to live our own lives, don't we?" he asked quickly.

She met his gray eyes. "Yes, I suppose we do."

"I believe these days they call it doing your own thing," he said with a smile.

"Yes," she laughed. "What about you? Don't you have any family?"

"Not much," he replied carefully. "At least, I seldom see them."

The percolator was bubbling and when it stopped, Sutton got up to pour the coffee.

"Everything's ready but the toast," Larina said. "Do you like it light or dark?"

"In between. Shall I fetch the trays? We could eat on the patio. I must say the sunsets are worth watching."

"It's an hour until sunset," she answered.

His gray eyes glowed. "I know. But we could wait for it, couldn't we?"

She didn't reply to that. But when he brought the trays, she arranged the two plates of food on them and he carried them out to the patio. It was comfortable there. Perhaps a bit more private than at Aunt Stell's and it looked toward the far end of the beach. She could even make out the roof of the Bleaker house.

Sutton devoured the food hungrily.

"Why don't you hire someone to fix your meals?" Larina asked.

He shook his head quickly. "No. I'd rather not have anyone around. I'm peculiar that way. I—I'm not an easy man to live with. I keep irregular hours. I'd drive a cook crazy within a week's time."

They laughed at that. Larina was aware that she had

come to like Sutton Ward. At times he was amusing as well as polite and thoughtful. He seemed genuinely pleased with her company and it was the kind of attention that could turn almost any woman's head. He was so totally different from John and she'd never known anyone like him before.

"Paint me a view of this, Larina, and I'll buy it," Sutton said with a sigh. "It is a very beautiful beach."

"But there are so many beautiful and interesting places in Florida."

"I haven't seen many. Perhaps someday, soon, I'll go sight-seeing. I'd like to visit Tarpon Springs. They gather sponges there. Should be interesting."

"Yes," she nodded.

"Would you come with me?" he asked in a quiet, hopeful voice.

"Who knows," she said. "I follow the wind!"

"Maybe you're just being a cautious young lady."

She felt the smile fade away from her face. Now, he was getting on dangerous ground, beginning to press too hard. Getting to her feet, she told him that she had to be going.

"So soon?"

"Yes."

There were footsteps inside the house. With a start, Larina turned about. A man stood there, partially in the shadows so that she couldn't see his face. Sutton leaped to his feet and his expression changed. All the warmth and charm was gone and was replaced with a cold hardness.

"I'll be with you in a moment," he said curtly to the intruder. "Please, wait inside."

Why was Sutton acting so strangely? Who was the man standing in the shadows and how had he got inside the house?

"Sorry," Sutton was saying.

He took her by the arm and walked with her to the edge of the patio.

"Thank you for everything, Larina. I'll see you tomorrow. On the beach. For shell hunting in the morning. All right?"

With a deep breath, she looked at the empty beach. At no other time of the day would it be so deserted.

Remembering Sutton Ward's promise to join her, she glanced toward his house. No light burned. He was probably sound asleep. Still, he had promised—

With a mischievous laugh, she decided to pay him a visit, roust him out. She half walked, half ran across the sand to the Bardwell house. Crossing the patio, she knocked at the glass doors. Peering inside, she couldn't see anyone stirring.

"Hey, Sutton! Sutton!"

She rattled the doors loudly, but either he was a sound sleeper or he wasn't there. Giving up at last, she turned away. She did hope the poor man wasn't ill. After her experience with him yesterday, it rather worried her.

Humming, greeting the sun with a smile, she went down to the water's edge. From somewhere, a small dog came bounding toward her, yipping and wagging his tail.

"Well, hello, pooch," Larina said. She bent down and rubbed his ears. In reply to her friendliness, he danced around her. Then as she proceeded on down the beach, he fell in step beside her. With every shell she retrieved, he was there, poking his nose against it, examining it.

"Okay, pooch? Shall I keep this one?"

They went on, a small young woman and a tiny dog, talking to each other, finding freshly washed shells, prodding out still others from the sand with a large broken conch.

After nearly an hour, she turned and went back toward Sea Mist. Returning to the house, she looked toward Sutton's place. But there was still no sign of life.

Aunt Stell was also an early riser and she was in the dining room in a fancy negligee, having her first cup of coffee.

"Good morning, Aunt Stell!"

"Hello, dear. Have any luck?"

"Not much. Maybe I'm getting too selective. How are you? How's your wrist?"

"Bothersome. But it will soon be as good as new. We

had an interesting meeting last night. Naturally most of it concerned the problem at Calley's."

"Still no new ideas?"

"No. The club is determined to raise money. But heaven knows how we'll ever manage to get all we need. The place needs so much work done: painting, new plumbing, goodness knows what all."

"I've tried to think of something unique, Aunt Stell, and I've come up blank! But I'll do my best."

Aunt Stell smiled. "I wish all our members had your enthusiasm."

"You enjoy your club work, don't you?"

Aunt Stell sighed heavily. "Yes. To a point. I hate being idle and with your uncle away—well, the days do get long. I wish Bert—"

"No word from him?"

"The last we knew, he was in Istanbul. What he was doing there, I haven't the vaguest idea! He dropped us a very short note saying he was going to Mexico next. Since that's just across the Gulf, I was hoping he'd spend some time here this summer."

"Maybe he will. I wish he would!" Larina said enthusiastically. "Bert and I always have so much fun together."

"Bert's been a disappointment to his father. Not that Ernie doesn't love him, he does. But Bert couldn't care less about being a banker and Ernie had hoped—"

"Bert will never be any more than what he is. A very carefree, country-hopping young man in search of fun, excitement, new faces, and new places."

"That's Bert. Sometimes, I think my sister was wrong to leave him all that money. But he is a grown man. We can't make him stay here."

"Bert will be home. Wait and see. He likes to fly from country to country, like a bee buzzing around the flowers, but he always comes home eventually—doesn't he? Like a bee to the hive?"

"That's an odd comparison," Aunt Stell smiled. "But, yes, you're right, Larina. He always comes home."

"I hope he comes while I'm here," Larina said wistfully.

"You're lonely, aren't you? You miss young people—"

"Oh, there's Tish and I like Lee Tyler. There's a new man in town, too. Nollie Oliver. He's fun."

"You've been to the playhouse?"

"Yes," Larina nodded. "I'm going to help them, Aunt Stell. With backdrops. I've never done anything like that, but I think it will be fun trying."

Aunt Stell patted her hand. "I'm glad you've made some new friends."

"I think I'll phone Dad. He'd ought to be having breakfast about now."

It took only a few seconds for the call to go through. Then she heard her father's gruff voice on the other end of the line.

"Hello, Dad! How are you?"

"Larina?" he asked with surprise. "Is something wrong?"

"No, Dad. Everything's fine. How are you?"

"I'm enduring," he replied with a laugh. "You sound happy."

"The weather and the beach are just perfect! Uncle Ernie got off on schedule and Aunt Stell sends her love. Dad, have you forwarded my mail?"

"Yes, I have. Wasn't much."

"Nothing from—"

"No. John hasn't written."

"Oh."

For a moment there was a pause on the line. Then Dad began talking quietly, asking questions, taking her mind off John Adair. After a few minutes, they said good-bye and hung up.

"Seems we both have a vagabond on our hands," Aunt Stell said kindly. "I have Bert, you have your John."

"Yes," Larina said, forcing the brightness into her voice.

"We'll just have to manage without them, won't we?"

Larina nodded. She wouldn't let the gloom settle over her heart. She wouldn't let any doubts or fears take hold. John was just busy or his letters hadn't had time to reach Riverdale or there was some good reason why she hadn't heard. He would make up for it when the summer was over. They would talk and talk and talk, just as they always had. They would be close, two heads together, two hearts in tune.

She shook away the last of her doubts. With a toss of her head, she blew Aunt Stell a kiss.

"I'm going next door."

"Next door? To Sutton's?"

"Yes. Oh, you didn't know about yesterday, did you? You're right. He does have a bad back. He had a kind of spasm yesterday and I had to help him home. I knocked on his door earlier and he didn't answer. I think I'd better go over again. Maybe he needs help."

Aunt Stell lifted her eyebrows. Then throwing her hands in the air, she laughed.

"Oh, run along, Larina. If the man is ill, just seeing your face will make him well."

Larina crossed the patio, stepped off into the sand and hurried next door. When she reached the Bardwell house, she knocked only a time or two and then she heard Sutton's footsteps. He seemed to be favoring his back more than ever.

When he saw her and slid open the glass doors, he was smiling happily.

"Good morning!"

"How are you, Sutton?"

"A little tired. Didn't sleep very well last night. You're just in time to make me some of that delicious coffee you brew."

"After you didn't show up on the beach this morning—"

He looked blank for a moment.

"I did promise, didn't I? And I would have been there, but my sleeping pill finally knocked me out. I haven't been up very long."

She cocked her head, hands on her hips and gave him a dubious look.

"I suppose I can forgive you this time. Just don't let it happen again."

"Will you stay? Have coffee?"

"This might get to be a habit."

His gray eyes glowed. "I should hope so. I think it's a great idea."

"I can't stay long. I want to paint the old Bleaker house today. Don't you think it would make a wonderful picture in oils?"

He stared at her. "What?"

"The Bleaker house. You know it. Up the beach."

"Oh, yes," he murmured. "But don't you find a place like that depressing? So old, deserted, lonely—"

"Interesting though. You know, I thought I saw a light there last night."

Sutton was just reaching for the coffee cups hanging inside the cupboard. One of them slipped and slammed to the floor, breaking into a dozen pieces.

"Awkward of me," he murmured.

"Let me help."

Kneeling together, they picked up the pieces of the broken cup.

"Did you ever see a light at the Bleaker house, Sutton?"

"No. Of course not!" he said quickly, almost angrily. "Everyone knows that no one has lived there for years!"

"Well, I decided it was just my imagination. But I wonder—oh well, it was probably nothing. I was at the playhouse last night. I told Lee Tyler about you. He said anytime you wanted to drop around—you'd be welcome."

"Oh, thank you, Larina. That was good of you."

"You still don't seem the type."

He got to his feet slowly, favoring his back. Then he reached out and with a subtle touch of his fingers to her cheek, he smiled at her.

"What type am I, Larina?"

She shook her head. "I don't know."

"Come with me to Tarpon Springs today. Maybe you'll get to know me better. It's only an hour or so by car."

"Not today."

"Tomorrow?"

She laughed and reached up for another cup.

"Perhaps."

"Larina—"

His gray eyes were watching her closely. Then with a little laugh, he shook his head.

"You're a great girl, Larina. I've never known anyone like you before."

She was looking at him steadily. Then making a frame with her hands, she began to smile happily.

"Of course! You're just perfect! Why didn't I think of it before?"

"Perfect for what?"

"Would you pose for me? I'd like to paint you."

He raised his brows in surprise. "Paint me?"

"Yes!" she said with excitement. "You're quite handsome you know. Such mysterious eyes!"

He laughed until he saw that she was serious.

"Would that mean we could spend a great deal of time together?"

"Portraits always take me longer. I'm quicker with scenery. Would you sit for me, Sutton? At my studio?"

"Only if you promise to make them long, long sessions and have them often."

She saw him take a step toward her. A light came on and off in his eyes. A warning bell sounded but it was a pleasant little jingle. She couldn't understand herself at all! Only a few moments ago, she had been unhappy because John hadn't written. Now, here she was practically inviting this man's attentions.

"Oh, dear," she murmured.

Then, suddenly, he swept her into his arms. He was stronger than she had expected. His cheek against hers was scratchy and warm.

"Ah, Larina—"

Then her good sense came back to her and she stepped out of his arms before he could kiss her.

"Coffee's ready," she said in a shaky voice.

"It would be. My timing is always off!" he said with lament.

"Let's have it on the patio. It's—it's safer there."

He smiled at that and got the tray.

"Think about Tarpon Springs. We'll make it an all-day outing. Tomorrow? Please?"

She was weakening. Without really meaning to, she heard herself saying yes. He nodded, pleased. Then with two brown hands, he reached for the tray.

"Coffee is served on the patio. Come along, dear girl."

IX

THE SUN WAS CLIMBING rapidly when Larina packed up
her paint box and easel, left her studio behind, and
trudged down the beach toward the Bleaker house. She
could have driven her car most of the way, but she
elected to walk. It gave her time to soak in the atmo-
sphere. In fact, she had been doing that so much, she
was beginning to feel waterlogged. But she loved every
minute spent looking at the sea.

There were a few people out strolling and Larina
smiled brightly to them and called good morning. By the
time she reached the Bleaker house, the easel was getting heavy.

"Ah! At last," she said.

Setting up the easel and putting her paint box down,
she stood for a long moment, nose wrinkled, eyes shad-
ed, staring at the old place. Sutton was right. It *was*
dreary. So out of place here on the sunlit beach. All the
houses were well cared for and the Bleaker house was
an eyesore in many respects.

"Oh, the stories you could tell me," she thought.

Leaving her easel, she decided she wanted a closer
look. Kicking sand ahead of her, she walked near the old
house. There was a wooden fence around it, such as it
was: neglect had taken its toll there. Debris had blown
and caught in its fallen boards. The house itself still held
a regal look despite its gray walls and high, narrow
windows. It was surely two and a half stories, easily the
tallest house on Beach Front Road.

"Hi!"

She looked up to see Nollie Oliver waving to her. He came dogtrotting toward her.

"Good morning, Nollie."

"What brings you?" he asked. "How come you're staring at that old place?"

"I'm going to paint it, Nollie."

Nollie made a face and rubbed a hand over his crew cut red hair.

"Shucks, thought maybe you came to find me. Now, I could really pose for you. How about like this? Or this?"

He began striking poses. "Coming by today? We've started getting the set ready for the first play."

"Perhaps later. I'll see. Now, Nollie, I have to get to work. Look how fast the sun's climbing!"

"Mind if I watch?"

"No," Larina laughed. "As long as you don't talk to me too much. It distracts me."

"I'll be like a mouse."

Nollie fell in step beside her as they walked back to her easel. She picked up her charcoal and began to rough in a sketch of the old house.

"What will you call it?"

"I don't know, Nollie. Depends on what kind of mood I manage to capture."

"Know anything about the place?"

"Not really. I understand some tragic things have happened there, but I don't know any details."

"Never expected to see a house like that on this beach," Nollie grinned. "Florida's great. Wish I had come sooner."

"Where's your home, Nollie?"

Nollie shook his head. "Nowhere. Everywhere. Wherever I am, that's home."

"You poor man! You mean you don't really have a home, a family somewhere?"

"No," he frowned. "Listen, I was born in Arkansas. On a dirt farm. My pa never had two dimes to rub together. I cut out when I was fourteen. Since then, everybody's scattered, folks are dead. I got nothin' and never did have anything."

"But don't you want things?"

Nollie rubbed a hand over his face and was sober for the first time. "Sure," he said in a low, angry voice. "Sure, I want things! I'd like to own any one of these houses along here. I'd like to have a jazzy car and more than one suit. I'd like a small mint in the bank! You know what, Larina, I'm going to have them too!"

She knew Nollie talked a great deal and didn't always follow a rational way of thinking. This was just more of his high-handed daydreaming.

"I'm sure you will, Nollie."

He laughed shortly. "Nobody believes me. But they'll see. Someday, they'll see. My ship will come in sometime soon—"

She glanced at the sea with a smile. "I don't see it, Nollie."

"No," he murmured. "I don't either."

She concentrated on her work then and Nollie left, but she didn't know when. The sun burned down on the top of her black hair. Maybe Uncle Ernie was right. She should purchase a beach hat. When the sun stood directly overhead, she picked up her things and headed back to Sea Mist. Bertha would be waiting lunch.

She didn't see anything of Sutton as she walked past the Bardwell house. The patio doors were closed. Perhaps he had gone out.

Lunch was light and appetizing. Aunt Stell fretted that Larina would get too much sun.

"You're going to get burned," she said anxiously.

"No. I'll come in when I get too warm. Perhaps this afternoon I'll work inside. I've got enough of the painting outlined that I believe I can finish there. Maybe I'll have to go back later for a few more details—"

After lunch, a spell of laziness attacked her so that she crawled onto a chaise longue on the patio and took a short nap. She heard a car next door and raised up in time to see Sutton driving away with a strange man. Who were those men that came so often to his house? With a shrug, Larina went to her studio and there she spent the afternoon, working happily, humming to herself. Overhead, she heard Nick in his room. Then he came down and she saw him working in the flowers.

The day sang along. The sky hadn't a cloud in it. The porpoise could be spotted off shore, leaping their way southward. White-winged gulls clustered on the beaches. Occasionally, someone would come out with a plate of old bread or scraps of food and they would go squawking there in a flutter of white wings to snatch the food as it was tossed, bit by bit, into the air.

Larina finished for the day, cleaned her brushes and stood back for a look at what she'd done. Nick rapped at her door and came in to give her a huge, red rose.

"It's beautiful, Nick. Thank you. How sweet of you to bring it!"

"What's that you painted?" Nick asked.

"The Bleaker house. What do you think, Nick?"

He scowled. "Why you up there snooping around?" he asked.

"I wasn't really snooping. Just looking. I guess you don't like it."

"Didn't mean it like that, Larina. Really, I didn't. Just don't like that Bleaker house. Never did. Eyesore. Somebody ought to tear it down."

"Perhaps they will," she said. "So, I'm glad to have it on canvas."

Nick made a face, waved good-bye and went back to his gardening.

The afternoon was dwindling. She thought of John with a wrench of her heart. Then with resolution, she put him out of her mind. Snapping on a small radio, she caught the last of a news broadcast. The announcer had been talking about the smuggling of drugs off the Florida coast. That in turn brought Jimmy Baker to mind.

There was time before dinner. Driving away, she made one stop at Tish's shop. There, she purchased a very large conch shell.

"I thought you had every kind of shell there was, Larina," Tish teased.

"This is for someone special."

"Coming by the playhouse tonight?"

"Perhaps I will," Larina promised.

She drove on to the Home and the minute the convertible came to a halt, she spied Jimmy. He was coming as fast as his short legs could carry him. As she stood waiting for him, he came to a sudden halt, nearly falling down. Then he stood there shyly, fists knotted.

"Hello, Jimmy!"

He didn't speak, but he held out his fist and opened it. The shell she'd given him was still there.

"Ah, Jimmy!" she laughed softly. "You kept it."

"A promise in my pocket," he said.

She was touched that he had remembered. Kneeling down, she smiled at him.

"And I didn't forget," she said. "Here. It's all wrapped up."

He tore into Tish's gift wrapping with eager fingers and soon the pink and white polished shell was in his hands. His brown eyes grew bigger and bigger.

"Hold it to your ear," Larina said. "Listen."

She showed him how to hold it and he listened, his mouth dropping open with the wonder of it.

"The sea," she told him. "It's captured all the sound of the sea!"

He insisted that she listen and for about ten minutes they did little else but take turns.

After that, she took him for a walk, away from the other children. His small hand nestled in hers and under a palm tree, they sat down, very close, and listened again to the shell.

"Someday, I'll see if I can arrange for you to go home with me. Maybe we can go swimming in the Gulf. And have a picnic. Bertha would bake us a chocolate cake. Would you like that?"

He nodded eagerly.

"My mommie and me went on a picnic once."

Larina bit her lip. "Did you?"

"It was fun."

Then the sadness was back in his face and his shoulders were drooping. For a moment, Larina was too touched to speak. What did she say? What did she do? But somehow, she found the right words and soon she had him laughing again. Then the bell was ringing. It was dinner time.

"You have to go in now, Jimmy."

"I don't want to. I don't want to! I want to go with you."

"You can't, Jimmy. But someday, someone will come and take you home with them. Somebody who wants a little boy like you very, very much."

"I'll get adopted?"

"Yes. You'll get adopted," Larina said. "You'll have a mommie again and a daddy. Maybe even a brother or sister. Wouldn't that be nice?"

He was clouding up again.

"I want to go with you!"

"You can't, Jimmy. But I'll come see you again."

"Even if I get adopted?"

She laughed and nodded. "Yes, Jimmy. Even if you get adopted!"

She walked with him to the door. All the others had gone inside. He was going to be late if he didn't hurry.

"See you soon," she said. "Good-bye."

She turned to walk back to the car and she heard him running toward her. But she was surprised when he caught her around the legs and gave her a tremendous hug. She held him close for a moment and then sent him on his way.

At the door, he turned for one last look and waved. But it was the smile on his face, a big, beaming smile, that somehow made the day for her. With a happy sigh, she drove away and went back to Sea Mist. She told Aunt Stell about her visit over dinner.

"Don't get too close, Larina. You'll be hurt."

She nodded. "I know. Maybe I already am. He—he talked about his mother today. Oh, I hate the people who started her on drugs! I hate the pushers, the people who buy and sell drugs to people like Jimmy's mother!"

Dinner was leisurely. She had promised Tish she would drop by the playhouse and she drove there about eight o'clock. She hadn't met all the people who were involved in the production, but she saw several familiar faces.

Lee was everywhere, shouting this, pointing at that, demanding perfection. But there was something magical about the stage, nearly barren, bathed in a harsh light, as people suddenly took on a new identity.

"Hello!"

She turned about.

"Angela Jones!" Larina said in surprise. "How are you?"

"I'm fine. I'd heard you were here for the summer. Are you interested in our play?"

"Yes. Very. I think it's all so exciting. Are you taking part in it, Angela?"

"You know me. I was hit with the acting bug as a kid. I've never recovered. And Lee's so good at directing. It's fun working with him."

"Oh?"

"When I heard the theatre was going to reopen, I was the first one here, waiting to volunteer my services."

"Angel, where are you?" Lee was calling. "Angel—"

"That's me," Angela laughed. "They all call me Angel around here. Isn't that silly?"

She rushed away and climbed the steps to the stage. There Lee patiently directed her.

Then at last, the rehearsal was over. To Larina it all seemed a mishmash with no logical order. But Lee seemed pleased. She spoke to him briefly.

"Glad you came," he said. "When will you come and work on the sets?"

"Soon," she promised.

Lee's hazel eyes flickered. "I hope so."

The next day, she was to go to Tarpon Springs with Sutton Ward and she was looking forward to it. He had promised they would get an early start, spend the day. In the morning, as she dressed, she was surprised to find how anxious she was to go. When the phone rang, Bertha said it was for her.

"Good morning, Larina."

"Sutton?"

"Yes. Larina, I hate this like everything. But . . . I'm away from the house and . . . I won't be able to take you to Tarpon Springs today. I'm sorry."

"Sutton, where are you?"

"Out of town. Business," he said with a curtness that

surprised her. "I'll see you when I get back. I really am sorry. You'll give me a rain check on it, won't you? Good-bye."

The line clicked and then went dead. With a sense of uneasiness, she hung up.

"The date's off, Aunt Stell," she said. "He just canceled out."

Aunt Stell was pouring her morning coffee. "Too bad. But somehow I get the feeling that Mr. Ward is not too reliable."

Larina wondered why he had done that. Business he'd said.

"I know!" she said, her face lighting. "I'm sure he's gone to see a doctor somewhere. His back has been bothering him so much and he's very sensitive about it, so that's why he didn't tell me what he's doing!"

"Perhaps that's it," Aunt Stell nodded. "So, what will you do now?"

"I should work on the Bleaker painting, but I think I'll go to the playhouse. I've been promising Lee to help with the work there and time's running out."

"I've another committee meeting this afternoon," Aunt Stell said. "So, I won't see you until evening."

Dressing in some paint-stained slacks and an old pair of sneakers, Larina drove once again to the playhouse.

Angela Jones was there. She had met Angela a couple of years ago. She was the daughter of one of Aunt Stell's friends. She had seemed nice enough, even friendlier than most, but for some reason Larina couldn't quite put a finger on, she didn't really like the girl. Right now, Angela was fawning over Lee. Lee seemed to take it in his stride. When he caught sight of Larina, he waved and motioned for her to join them.

"Angel, Nollie needs a hand over there. Why don't you go and help him? I'll get Larina started on some backdrops. I'm surely glad to see you, Larina."

"I had a change of plans. So I'm at your disposal, all day," she told him. "What's first?"

"Over here."

There seemed to be no end to the work to do. Everyone was aware that the first performance would be taking place soon and that everything, absolutely everything, had to be ready for that. But it was fun. Larina liked the few who had come to help and Lee was very attentive. Nollie kept everyone in stitches and yet managed to get a fair-sized amount of work done, too.

Larina had never painted such a large area before, but she was pleased to see that it was coming along nicely.

"I can almost smell the green leaves on that tree," Lee said with a grin. "And do I hear a frog croaking over there by the creek?"

"No. You hear *two* frogs!"

Lee checked his watch. "Lunchtime. Will you join me? I have the makings of a sandwich in my tiny refrigerator."

"I'd like that," she nodded.

Cleaning the brushes and wiping the paint off her hands, she left the stage with him.

"I've a better idea," Lee said. "How about a picnic? On the beach?"

"Fine," she said.

"Give me a minute to gather up some food."

"Let me help."

Half an hour later, they were going to the beach, a large paper bag and a thermos jug in tow. Lee found a secluded spot near the water, spread an old blanket and Larina got out the food. They ate hungrily, saying very little. When the food was gone, Lee stretched out, arms under his head and watched the sky. The sun seemed to erase the tense lines about his mouth. He closed his eyes and seemed to be asleep.

Taking a paper napkin, Larina leaned over him carefully and tickled his nose. He opened his eyes and made a lunge at her. She laughed and fell back.

"I'll teach you not to fool with me!" he said.

With a screech, she began to run pell-mell down the beach. But he was close behind her. In a few seconds he had caught her. With a playful motion, he picked her up in his arms and pretended to toss her into the surf.

"Let me down, let me down!"

She pounded his heavy shoulders with her fists. But he only laughed and held her tighter.

"Let me down!"

"For a price," he said.

"What price?" she asked suspiciously.

"One kiss."

Her heart did a queer little dance inside.

"Lee—"

"One little kiss."

Then he wasn't asking any more, he was taking. The kiss was longer than the first one he'd given her and she pulled quickly out of his arms.

"Oh, Lee—"

"Let it happen, Larina. Why not? We've got the summer ahead of us. Why not make it mean something?"

"I don't go in for lighthearted love affairs—"

"Maybe it's time," he said quietly. "Maybe it's time, Larina."

X

Larina spent the afternoon working on the backdrop and every time Lee came near her, she was aware of him. He gave her a wink when he walked by, stopped to admire her work and in general was very attentive. No one seemed to notice except Angel Jones. She was constantly seeking Lee's advice about this or that. When everyone began to scatter at the supper hour, Lee asked Larina to stay. But she shook her head.

"Thank you. I think not. I really haven't been spending much time with my aunt and I know she's lonely. I'll see you later, Lee. Perhaps tomorrow."

Then with a wave of her hand, Larina said good-bye and hurried away. She was pleasantly tired from her work at the playhouse but it was the little episode on the beach that worried her. Lee was becoming too attentive. Too suggestive. Didn't he understand there was someone else in her life? She had told him. Had warned him. But somehow, it all seemed to bounce right off him like rain off a tiled roof.

"I'm all mixed up," Larina sighed. "So mixed up!"

As she drew near Sea Mist, she glanced at Sutton's house. His car was in the drive. He was home! Putting her own car in the garage, she decided to pay him a quick visit, just to reassure herself that he was all right. If he had been to the doctor, she would like to know what he'd said. She worried about Sutton, all alone there in such a big house!

She chose to go by way of the patio. As she crossed the stone floor noiselessly in her paint-stained sneakers, she heard voices inside. Sutton wasn't alone.

"I tell you, we'd ought to clear out!" the man was saying angrily. "Why are you so obstinate about this, Sutton?"

"I'm staying. I'm going to do what I came here to do! Is that clear?"

"I don't think it's smart. The boss doesn't think it's smart. They may be wise to us! Don't you understand that?"

"You're jumping to conclusions," Sutton replied in an even, firm voice. "There's no real grounds for that."

"You're on borrowed time, Sutton! Remember that!"

Larina couldn't understand what they were talking about, but there was something sinister in the tone of their voices. She paused midway on the patio. Obviously it would be best not to disturb Sutton now.

What had all that meant? She didn't know. She didn't really want to think about it.

That evening, she persuaded Nick to take her out on the *Mary Belle* for a short ride.

"She's a great little cruiser," Nick said proudly as he gave Larina a hand inside. "Where would you like to go?"

"Oh, up the beach, toward the playhouse. I might take a look at the Bleaker house, just to see how it seems from the sea. It might help me finish my painting."

Nick was whistling as he untied the mooring rope and gave the boat a little push away from the dock. Then with a roar, he started the motor. They darted away from the shore, the nose of the cruiser riding high. Larina let the sea wind blow against her face and she enjoyed the throb of the motor and the way the waves splashed across the bow just as much as Nick. Someday, she must bring Jimmy and have Nick take him for a ride.

Nick circled about and nosed the *Mary Belle* toward the shore again, slowed the motor and finally turned it off entirely. They drifted for a few minutes as she studied the Bleaker house. It rose tall and majestic above all the other houses. Despite the decay and neglect, the old house had something special.

"I'm afraid I haven't really done it justice, Nick."

"Why don't you paint something handsome, like me?" Nick teased.

"I *am* going to paint something handsome. Sutton Ward."

Nick arched his white brows at that and a frown cut across his forehead.

"Sutton Ward?"

"My goodness, you don't like him either?"

"Too fancy for me. No, I don't like him."

Larina told herself that she shouldn't like him either, but she did.

Nick cruised up and down the shore for nearly an hour before she told him she was ready to go in. With a sigh, Nick turned the *Mary Belle* toward home.

"I wish I was at sea again," he muttered.

"Do you really, Nick?"

"Had me some times in those days. Never knew from one day to the next what kind of a hassle I'd be in. Seen some real excitement. Yes sir, I sure did."

"And being a gardener is dull?"

"Dull," Nick nodded. "But about all that's left to me in my old age unless—"

"Unless?" she asked.

"You heard the news about the drug smugglers? They think they're off the Florida coast, maybe somewhere in this area!"

"I heard something about it on the radio and it gives me the shivers, just thinking about it."

"You know what I'd like to do? Catch them red-handed, turn them over to the police!"

"I wish you could too, Nick! Oh, how I wish you could!"

She thought about Jimmy and what had happened to him because of people just like the smugglers. Nick tied up the boat and they walked back to Sea Mist. Nick disappeared toward his room over the garage. Aunt Stell was writing a letter to Uncle Ernie.

Larina was restless. She could always go to the playhouse and watch rehearsals, but she didn't want to do that. It was too late to visit Jimmy.

"Would you like to go for a ride, Aunt Stella?" she asked. "Perhaps up the coast?"

Aunt Stell put her pen aside. "I believe I would. I'll only be a moment."

When Larina got the convertible out of the garage, she wondered if she and Sutton would ever visit Tarpon Springs together. Perhaps she should plan a few outings and take Aunt Stell with her, even though her aunt had already seen most of the sights many times. Maybe Jimmy could join them. A girl couldn't work constantly. It made her dull!

Aunt Stell appeared and they drove away from Sea Mist. Leaving the town of Gull Haven behind, they drove down the highway. Aunt Stell didn't like her hair to blow in the open convertible, so she had put on a scarf. The wind didn't worry Larina. She liked it and her short hair didn't suffer from it.

"Where are we going?" Aunt Stell asked.

"Remember the Peterson Orange Grove?"

"We used to go there. But lately, Ernie and I haven't been out there. Just got out of the habit I guess."

"Well, Bert and I used to come all the time. I'd just like to see them again."

"Bert," Aunt Stell said sadly. "Still no word from him. What can he be doing in Mexico?"

"Whatever it is, I'm sure he's having a grand time, Aunt Stell! Bert could always find excitement and fun."

"I worry about him," Aunt Stell confessed. "I'm afraid he's a good deal like Sutton Ward. Just a playboy! Spending money like water but doing nothing to earn it. Just—just wasting his life away!"

Larina turned the car toward the Peterson Orange Grove. She saw the green twisted orange trees, some of them very tall. It seemed they had grown quite a lot since she and Bert had come here.

"Pete suffered a severe loss last winter," Aunt Stell said "We had a cold snap and the trees were nipped by frost. Such a shame. Pete works so hard. But being an orange grower is sometimes a risky business."

"Bert showed me once how they picked oranges, sorted them, washed them, packed them, shipped them. Quite an industry."

"I'm surprised Bert took that much interest," Aunt Stell said wryly.

Bouncing along the sandy lane, they followed Peterson's grove of trees. There was no light in the house at the end of the lane and the packing sheds were dark.

"No one's home. I'll drop by another time," Larina said.

Driving back to Gull Haven, she persuaded her aunt to stop at a drive-in with her and they ordered cold lemonade. Snapping on the radio, they heard a newscast.

"Authorities are closing in on the ring of drug smugglers operating off the Florida Gulf Coast. A reported shipment that was to have arrived two days ago did not materialize, leading to speculation that there never was such a shipment or that the smugglers had been tipped off that police were waiting for them. Over the past six months an estimated two million dollars worth of drugs have arrived through some point on the Gulf Coast. Police are still hopeful—"

Larina snapped off the radio. It seemed she could hear nothing else on the radio and the whole town was in a stir about it.

Driving back to Sea Mist, Larina drove slowly down Beach Front Road, reluctant to reach the house. The evening was still young. There had been no letter from John. She knew it was useless to phone Dad again. The plain and simple truth was that John had not written and perhaps would not write at all. The thought made her feel all the more restless and lonely.

"I wish Bert would come back," Larina sighed. "We always had so much fun."

Aunt Stell didn't reply. Her silence told Larina that she understood how lonely she felt. But she didn't press her to talk about John and she was grateful for that. Somehow, she couldn't really tell anyone about him.

Oh, but it would work out! She was sure of it! Once the summer was over and she was back at Riverdale High, things would fall back to their proper perspective.

Meanwhile, she had the summer to make as busy as she could.

Lee was proposing a light love affair. A summertime romance. With no strings. Although he hadn't said it just like that, it was what he had meant. He wanted her to think about it. And it might be fun. Dating Lee. Being a part of his life, his work, his ideals. Lee was not a shallow man, but a deep, intelligent, moody, very romantic sort.

They had reached Sea Mist. As Larina turned into the drive, she thought she saw someone dart back into the shadows.

"Aunt Stell—"

"Yes?"

Aunt Stell hadn't seen anything. Perhaps it had been a prowler, even a burglar! For a moment, Larina's heart went to her mouth.

"Oh, nothing," Larina said.

She drove into the garage and they went inside. At the door, Larina looked around cautiously. Perhaps it was only her imagination. With all the talk on the radio about the smugglers and the police, her nerves were just edgy.

Aunt Stell went back to her room and her unfinished letter. For a little while, Larina watched a movie on the television. It wasn't late when she finally went upstairs. Getting ready for bed, she put out the light and went to the window, watching the sea for a little while. To the north, she saw a light burning in Sutton's house.

What about Sutton Ward? Nice. Attractive. Irresistible. Or was he something else? A cold, hard-voiced man whom no one seemed to like but her? For a moment, she remembered the way Sutton had put his arms around her, the warm, scratchy surface of his cheek against her own. It made her feel somehow protected, not so lonely, almost happy.

Strange! She hardly knew Sutton Ward. Yet, there was a glow about him that she could warm her heart by.

She couldn't sleep. Turning about, she tried to think of her work, of Jimmy, of John, of anything but Sutton

Ward. She heard Aunt Stell go to bed and the house became quiet and dark.

What was that! With a start, Larina sat up in bed. Something at the window! But how could that be when she was on the second floor?

Once again she heard something rattling against the screen. With a leaping pulse, she got up, thrust her feet into her slippers and inched toward the window for a better look. There! Someone on the patio, nearly hidden in the shadows. Pebbles tapped against her screen. Someone wanted her. Secretly. But who? Why like this? Why not simply go to the door and ring the bell?

She put her head out the window.

"Who's there?" she called.

"Sh! Sh!"

Then the man revealed himself. Her eyes widened with surprise. He motioned wildly for silence.

"Come down," he called softly. "Quietly!"

"All right."

She reached for a robe, pulled it on and silently opened her door. She listened for a moment. No sound, only the muffled thunder of the tide coming in.

Feeling like a prowler in her own house, she slipped down the stairs, careful of one squeaky step. Then crossing the hall to the dining room, she edged up to the glass doors and eased them open.

She paused for a moment, looking for him. But he was nowhere in sight. Stepping out to the patio, she called softly.

"Where are you?"

"Over here. I'll join you on the beach, away from the house!"

"But why—"

He had gone. She saw his slim, lithe figure slip back into the darkness. Kicking off her slippers, she stepped barefoot into the sand. She walked toward the water and waited there.

Then at last, she saw him coming from down the beach, running at an easy gait.

"Hello, Larina. Thanks for coming."

"Bert! What in the name ... ? Why are you dressed like that? Are you growing a beard?"

"What's this?" he asked in his usual lighthearted voice. "Just questions? No hug and kiss for your favorite cousin?"

"Oh, Bert! You've worried Aunt Stell half to death! Where have you been? Why are you acting like this?"

He laughed and gave her a quick hug. "Do me a favor, will you? Fetch me some clothes from my room. A little cash. And a razor. On the double and on the QT. Will you do that, Larina? Please?"

"Bert, what's wrong? What's happened?"

"I'm in a peck of trouble. Now, I can't tell you any more than that."

"Oh, Bert!"

"Will you help me, Larina? Please? You're the only one I can trust and I don't want to worry Mother. Will you?"

XI

"Bert, you've got to tell me what's going on!"

"Look, I just got into a little jam in Mexico and well—I had to clear out in a hurry and leave everything behind."

"What kind of trouble, Bert?"

He dropped an arm around her shoulder and tugged her along the beach.

"Nothing you'd understand. Really. It's all very complicated. Listen, I just need some help and I was hiding in the garage when you came home earlier—I thought I could catch you then—but I saw Mother was with you."

"Then I didn't just imagine someone was hiding there—"

"No, it was me," Bert laughed. "The house was locked and I couldn't get in and besides, I didn't really want Bertha and Nick to know I was around. What they don't know won't hurt them."

"Bert, you're not making a bit of sense!"

"I never did, did I?" he asked. "Now, will you help me?"

"Of course! You know I will, but I just don't understand—"

"I'll wait out by the patio, in the shadows. Slip in and get the things and hurry back."

"But why don't you just stay here? Why are you going to leave again?"

"Just trust me, Larina."

She sighed. There never was a time when she wouldn't give in to Bert. He could charm her into doing almost anything. They moved back toward Sea Mist and Bert slipped away to the shadows.

Quietly, Larina let herself back inside the house. Then going up the carpeted stairs, she moved quickly down the hall to Bert's room. There, she closed the door and risked a light. Finding a small bag in the closet, she filled it with as many clothes as she could cram into it, raided his bathroom for a spare razor and then went to find her purse in her own room. From it, she took all the cash she had.

Slipping back downstairs, she crossed the patio to the shadows.

"Bert—"

"Thanks, honey," Bert said, taking the things from her hand. "You're a lifesaver."

"Where will you be? How can I reach you?"

"I'll be in touch. Now, don't worry and not a word to Mother, okay?"

"But Bert—"

Then he was gone, moving away with swift steps, staying in the shadows, until he had disappeared from sight. Larina pulled her robe around her a little closer, somehow feeling a chill. What was going on anyway? What had Bert Goodwin done this time?

With a shake of her head, she went back inside and up to her room. Her sleep was shattered now. Finally, she snapped on a light and read until she grew drowsy again.

She overslept the next morning, so that by the time she had taken her plastic pail and headed for the beach on her usual shell-hunting walk, the sun was already up.

"Larina!"

She was surprised to find Sutton Ward strolling toward her, wearing casual slacks and canvas shoes, a sports shirt open at the neck. She always forgot how attractive he really was.

"Good morning, Sutton."

He fell in step beside her. "Mad at me?" he asked.

"No."

"I'm really sorry about breaking our date for Tarpon Springs. Let's go today."

"I—I should finish my painting."

"Please? I'd like to make it up to you. Something came up and I just couldn't get back in time yesterday."

She wondered if he was going to tell her now about seeing a doctor. But he made no further explanation.

"How's your back?" she asked.

"Better," he replied. "Much better. Now, Tarpon Springs?"

The sun made the shine of his black hair as glossy as a crow's wings and his gray eyes reflected the sea, stormy one moment, quiet the next.

"All right, Sutton. I'd love to go. I really would! I've heard so much about it and I've never been there."

"Nor have I. We'll discover it together. Shall we leave in a couple of hours?"

"Fine."

They made their morning walk along the beach a short one and parted a few minutes later. Larina ate a quick breakfast. Aunt Stell was sleeping late and she was rather glad of it. How could she *not* tell Aunt Stell about Bert being back?

Larina chose the green dress that accented her dark hair, put on a pair of high-heeled white shoes and chose a white purse. By the time she was ready, Sutton was waiting for her on the patio.

"I'm going to enjoy this. I'm not going to think about anything but having fun."

"I thought that was your main concern in life," she teased.

"Yes. I suppose it is. But since my surgery, I haven't had much fun. I'm glad you came to Gull Haven this summer, Larina."

Sutton drove a long, low sports car, befitting a man like him, and it was fun to climb in, fasten the seat belt, and whisk away down Beach Front Road. The sun was warm and bright with a brilliance typical of Florida in the summer. Larina had picked up a golden tan from her hours on the beach and it gave her a radiant look.

It was nearly a two hour drive from Gull Haven to Tarpon Springs and Sutton talked about many things as he pushed the sports car down the highway. He asked a great many questions about her work and her classes at Riverdale High.

"I didn't know school teachers came so pretty," he told her with his slow smile. "Mine were all a hundred and four with knots of hair on the back of their heads and wore bifocals."

"The world has changed," she replied with a laugh. "There are a great many young teachers these days."

"Do you enjoy your work?"

"Very much."

"Wouldn't you rather be a free-lance artist?"

"It would be fun. But I have to be practical too. How many paintings could I hope to sell?"

"Yes, I suppose you're right."

"That's probably something you don't really understand."

"How do you mean?"

"The working class must work."

He arched his brows at that and gave her a crooked smile. "Oh, yes, I understand that."

"I'm not sure, Sutton. No offense intended."

"I'm just one of the filthy rich with no destination in mind, making no contribution to society, is that it?"

Larina was embarrassed that he had put it so plainly into words. But it was what Uncle Ernie had said and she was afraid he was right.

"Does that bother **you**?" Sutton asked anxiously. "Do you dislike me for it?"

She thought for a moment and then turned back to him with a happy smile. "No, Sutton, I don't! Not really. I find you—"

"Don't stop there," he said. "Please, continue—"

"All right," she said, feeling a little reckless. "I find you interesting and charming, if a bit puzzling at times."

"I want us to be friends, Larina. Good friends."

"We are," she said with a shrug.

"Thank you."

Soon they had reached the junction and they left the busy north and south highway to turn west to the coast once again and Tarpon Springs.

Finding their way to the docks, they left the car in a

parking lot and walked toward the sponge boats. The town was a line of souvenir shops and restaurants on one side with the bay on the other.

"Get your tickets here. See a diver go down for sponges!"

Sutton looked at her. "Shall we?"

"Sounds like fun. Yes, let's do it all!"

So, Sutton purchased the tickets and in a few minutes, they were aboard the boat with several other people. With a chug, chug, chug of the motor, they moved slowly away from the docks, past many other sponge boats and a few shrimp boats and into the open water.

The diver was a man with a brown, lined face, sitting in his weighted shoes and rubber suit, waiting to put on the helmet and go over the side of the boat.

The boat came to a halt. Several were taking pictures of the diver as he prepared to go into the water and Larina wished she'd had presence of mind to bring her camera. Checking the air hoses, taking a hook and net with him, the diver slid out of view and disappeared into the water.

"I wouldn't like his job!" Larina said with a shiver.

"But it must be a fascinating world on the bottom of the ocean."

Larina watched anxiously, waiting for the diver to surface again. Several minutes passed. It seemed an eternity to Larina.

"Here he comes! He's got one!"

Soon, the diver was being reeled in. He held up his net triumphantly with a sponge rested inside.

Larina was conscious of heaving a sigh of relief. Sutton reached out and gripped her hand.

"See, he's all right."

Once the diver was in the boat again and his helmet was removed, he passed the sponge around for them all to see. The man running the boat told them over a loudspeaker about the various kinds of sponges found here. Some were called sheepswool, reef, yellow, or glove sponges and he showed them samples of each. They heard about the auction sheds, the way the sponges were sorted, cleaned, and bleached.

The boat had them back in about thirty minutes and Sutton helped Larina off at the dock. They wandered on down the street, stopping often to peer into the souvenir shops, where there was every sort of knickknack imaginable. She made one purchase—a small toy boat for Jimmy.

"What would you like? I'll buy it for you," Sutton said.

"I don't know. Some memento, anything," she answered. "So I can remember the day."

"We'll keep looking until we find the exactly right thing."

Farther down the street, they saw sponges hanging in great bunches, dozens in a string, some of them very large and yellow. Sponges were everywhere, all kinds, all sizes, sitting in boxes, piled on sidewalk tables or heaped in baskets. There were a great many Greek-Americans here and they operated the sponge boats and most of the souvenir shops as well as several restaurants.

By the time Sutton and Larina had looked into some of the stores, it was lunchtime and they found their way into one of the restaurants. There, they ordered strange-sounding Greek dishes, and Sutton was amused at her open excitement.

"You have so much fun out of little things."

She laughed. "Why not? Why waste life by going around with a long face?"

"But life can't always be a picnic or an excursion to Tarpon Springs," he said with a frown.

"No," she replied. "I suppose you've heard all the news about the drug smugglers off the Florida coast?"

Sutton met her eyes for a long moment. "Yes, of course. It's been in the paper, on the television—everywhere."

"There's that side of the world too, but I don't like thinking about it. I—I hate anyone who has anything to do with the drug market!"

Sutton leaned back, an odd look on his face. "Do you?"

"Yes!" she said vehemently.

By then, the waitress was there and Larina forgot

about the drug smugglers and concentrated on the different but delicious food on her plate.

They spent over an hour there, eating leisurely, dawdling over their coffee and dessert. Sutton's gray eyes had a way of disarming her.

Once more out in the street and searching through the shops, Sutton found a small figurine of a sea gull that was exquisitely made and he bought it for her.

"To remember our hours in Florida on the beach," he said. "And today."

"Thank you. I'll always keep it."

They spent much of that afternoon there, wandering about, talking, having cold drinks and munching Greek pastry in a bakery. Then almost reluctantly, they decided it was time to go back to Gull Haven. Sutton didn't drive fast, as if he wanted to hold back the day and the arrival home. He reached out a hand and took hers.

"Larina, come closer—"

"Sutton—"

"All right. I won't rush you. I suppose this isn't the time or the place."

He let go of her hand and to her surprise, pulled off the busy highway under a twisted old pine tree with Spanish moss waving in the breeze from its branches.

He turned to her. His gray eyes were warm and tender.

"Larina, I've never known a girl like you. I didn't really think anyone like you existed in this sordid old world. Then one day, I opened my eyes on the beach and there you were."

He moved closer and reached out to put his arms around her. Perhaps the day had been too much for her. It had been fun, different, even exciting. She felt alive and at peace with the world. She had been under the spell of Sutton's charms for hours and it had left her vulnerable, aware of her loneliness, aware of her needs.

"Oh, Sutton—"

He was kissing her then. His lips were warm and firm against hers. Almost against her will, she put her arms around him and gave him back his kiss.

"Larina, I'm falling in love with you."

"No. You mustn't!" she said with a shake of her head.

"How do you stop it? It's like being on a roller coaster and on the downhill slide. It's picking up speed all the time and the faster I go, the more I'm unable to stop it."

"But, Sutton—"

"I'm sure there's someone else in your life, even if you haven't told me so. I can't help that. I have to be selfish at this point. I have to think of myself. Believe me, Larina, I've never really loved a woman before. Not really."

"But you've been so many places, seen so much, done so much, surely known a great many women—"

"All kinds and shapes, but none were ever like you."

Then he was kissing her again and she didn't care that passing motorists were gawking at them in amusement. She didn't care that she suddenly lost all her good sense. She only knew that the man in her arms was awakening new sensations in her, new, deeper emotions.

"Oh, Sutton."

"Fall in love with me, Larina. Please, fall in love with me!"

XII

BERT GOODWIN HAD SPENT the day hiding in an orange grove near town. He'd used a public rest room to clean up and change his clothes. But after a second thought, he'd left his beard as it was, itchy and not too attractive, but a good disguise. The trouble was, he was widely known around Gull Haven. Right now, he didn't want to run into any old friends or answer any questions. He just wanted to be incognito. He only hoped Larina wouldn't spill the beans to his mother. But Larina was a good scout and they'd been friends too long. She'd stick by him. He was sure of that.

When night came, Bert risked going into an obscure diner on the edge of town, ate hungrily, paid the check from the meager cash Larina had given him and left quickly.

It was a long hike to Beach Front Road, but he couldn't risk a taxi or even riding the public bus. He'd played with fire just once too often and he'd got burned, in fact he'd nearly gotten exterminated altogether. Those boys weren't playing marbles in Mexico.

"I always put my nose in the wrong places," Bert thought, making a wry face.

But before, it had always been fun. Stirring up excitement was his second name. It was how he'd gone through life. Going from one experience to the next, having a ball. Mexico had been fine, up to a point. Up to that fatal night. He didn't want to remember. It was best to think ahead, work out his plans. It was time to play the little game of getting even, and he was determined to do it. As soon as he could, he got down to the beach.

Everyone walked there. He was probably less conspicuous there than on the streets.

It was just dusk. The sky was turning purple, pink, and red, bathing the ocean with the same rosy color. He took a moment to breathe deeply, to stare out at the boats coming back to shore, at the larger ships farther out.

The beach ran nearly the length of Gull Haven and he had a long walk. By the time he was nearing home, it was dark. He no longer felt as if everyone was staring at him and recognizing him. With a sense of longing, he thought of his room upstairs at Sea Mist, of a warm shower, a good shave and one of Bertha's special dinners. But that wasn't for him. Not until he'd settled a few things.

He walked swiftly along the water, passed the dock where the *Mary Belle* rocked gently and hurried on. All the houses had lights in their windows and occasionally, he met someone walking along the beach. Then he would bend quickly as if to tie a shoe or stand with his back to them, shoulders hunched, praying no one would recognize him.

Then at last, he saw the old house, outlined against the sky, paint faded, the crumbling fence cluttered with litter.

How to get in? Well, he had to try. Slowly, careful to stay in the shadows, he circled the house, pausing every few seconds to listen and look. But if there was anyone around, he could not spot them. Maybe he was on the wrong trail. But he'd have a look inside to be sure.

Next door, several yards away, he saw the old inn ablaze with lights. The playhouse had been reopened. Cars were beginning to come and he heard people shouting to each other. Inside, he heard the sound of hammering. Then it grew quiet and he guessed they were holding rehearsals.

Every window seemed securely locked. Every door had been padlocked shut and was intact. But by a stroke of luck, he noticed the straggly brush that had grown up around the house had been trampled down near a basement window. His senses picked up with a little excited quirk and dropping to his knees, he pushed on the basement window. It creaked open. He'd found the way in!

"Someone's been here before," he muttered to himself. "I'm on the right track."

He eased himself, feet first, into the window and touched a table that would support his weight. Then climbing down from that, he risked his flashlight for a moment. Finding the stairway, he crept up it slowly, quietly.

There was enough light coming in the windows, that he could grope his way about, mindful to make no noise, although he doubted anyone passing by could hear him inside. The surf muffled everything else, for it was stronger here and closer to the house than at Sea Mist.

Finding a window that looked out to the Gulf, he stood there, staring out to the black water. There was nothing unusual. No signaling lights. But then, it was early. It might not be the right night. The thing to do was wait. All night if necessary.

Resigned to that, he made himself as comfortable as possible and hoped it wouldn't be in vain.

The minutes ticked away slowly. Once, he thought he heard a sound in the house and decided it was just the old place creaking in the sea breeze. Now and then, he saw people strolling by on the beach. The lights at the playhouse were still on. A car started. Another. People were leaving. Looking at the luminous numbers on his watch, he saw he'd been here nearly three hours.

A familiar sound greeted his ears. With surprise, he got to his knees and peered out the window again. It was the *Mary Belle*! He'd know that motor anywhere. Was Larina having Nick take her for a ride? Or was that old scoundrel out joyriding just for himself?

Bert grinned thinking about Nick.

"I'd die if I wasn't within spittin' distance of the sea," Nick always told him. "Yes sir, I'd just curl up my toes and die."

Bert often suspected that Nick used the boat for his own personal pleasure when they happened to be away. Mother was probably home tonight, but didn't realize what Nick was up to. As for Dad, Nick didn't pull the wool over his eyes. But Dad was away, in Europe. What better time for the mouse to play than when the cat was away?

Bert grinned thinking about it. He stifled a yawn.

"This is getting boring!" he thought.

He liked more action, more life, more stirring. But waiting for an unknown boat that would arrive at an unknown time, demanded patience, perseverance and a great deal of luck. He might even be at the wrong contact point! But he didn't think so. It all pointed to the old Bleaker house. The other contacts had been made up or down the gulf at other spots, some in remote areas. He knew that much. But the one big haul was to be here. On sleepy little Gull Haven Beach! He couldn't believe it! The old town would never recover from the shock. He wondered why they had chosen such a conspicuous place? Yet there was safety and obscurity in numbers.

It seemed he could pick out the motor of the *Mary Belle* cruising around for about an hour. Then he heard it head back toward the home dock. Soon the sound was gone. Nick had taken the boat home. Getting stiffly to his feet, Bert paced about for a few minutes, loosening his tired muscles. The sandy soil of an orange grove hadn't made the best of beds last night.

What was that? Like a startled animal, he swung about, ears trained for the least little sound. Had he heard something below him, the thumping of the basement window being opened and reclosed? Tense, nerves coiled, he waited, clenched his hand tightly around his flashlight, wishing mightily that he'd had brains enough to have brought some kind of weapon with him.

There were unmistakable steps on the stairs now, the creaking of the door opening.

It could only be one of them! The contact man! Maybe tonight was the night!

"Steady, boy," Bert told himself. "Steady!"

The steps were coming toward him and they were coming without hesitation, as if whoever it was knew his way around in the old house.

Then abruptly the steps stopped. A light came on and

shone straight into Bert's eyes. He gave a yell and plunged at the light. It was knocked to the floor and went out. Bert had his hands full. The guy was quick, tough and he fought like a tiger. Bert grabbed hold of his shirt and a bit of material ripped off into his fist. Then there was a blow to Bert's midsection that robbed him of his breath, followed by something that was surely a karate chop. Bert stumbled to the floor and caught himself on his hands and knees, shaking his head to clear it, gulping for air. Then there was another blow, and with a groan, Bert collapsed to the floor in an untidy heap. There were strange, whirling lights before his eyes, a roar in his ears, and then only blackness.

Bert had no idea how long he had been unconscious. When he came around, he smelled the dust on the floor and tasted blood in his mouth. Then getting up slowly, he remembered where he was and why he was here. He'd tipped them off! Fool! Fool!

Struggling to his feet, his one thought was to get out of the house, into the safety of the warm, black night. With effort, he found his way through the dark house to the basement stairs and groped his way to the window. Hoisting himself up, he managed to wiggle out. The fresh air helped his throbbing head and he had presence of mind to proceed slowly.

He would never be able to make it back to the orange grove. Where could he go. Home? Out of the question. Unless—maybe Larina could help him again. Drive him somewhere. Suggest a place for him to go.

He began walking, nearly stumbling, his ribs aching from the blow he'd taken and his head roaring. Going down to the water, he scooped up handfuls of it and bathed his face. It left a sticky, salty residue but he felt better. Sea Mist seemed miles away. But he pushed on, trying to walk faster.

Sea Mist was in sight now at last. He began to breathe a little easier. Two people were coming toward him. He paused and turned to the sea, hoping they would go on by without speaking or even really noticing him.

Then suddenly, two men were on either side of him, pinning his arms behind him.

"All right. You'd better come along."

"What is this? Who are you?"

There were no answers to his questions, just strong arms holding him and the unmistakable feel of a pistol in the small of his back.

"March," came a curt, no-nonsense voice. "March!"

"Let me go!" Bert demanded. "I'll yell my head off. What do you want, money? I haven't got any. Let me go!"

"Be quiet. You've a gun in your back and I wouldn't want to have to use it. There's a few questions we want to ask you. Now, come quietly, if you know what's good for you."

"Who are you?"

There was no answer. He hadn't expected any. They were taking him away from the beach, toward the houses that sat in such a neat row on the shore.

"Where are you taking me?" he demanded again.

"You'll find out, and when we get there, mister, you'd better be prepared to talk."

"What is this, a gag? I'm just walking along, minding my own business and out of the blue—"

He tried to make a joke of it. He had talked himself out of more than one tight spot in his life. But try as he did now, it didn't work.

He felt sick, bruised, battered. But he had to keep his wits about him. Whoever had beat him up in the old Bleaker house had sent word to these two punks to pick him up and take him somewhere for questioning. For more beatings? For possibly—

He felt sick. Greenish sick. Like that time as a kid when Nick had taken him out to sea in a small boat and a storm had caught them. Nick never believed in small-craft warnings. He always said he could ride out anything God wanted to dish up to him. Now, he had to do that. He had to ride the thing out. Use every sense and wit and scheme and trick in the book. What good would he do anybody dead?

They led him through an opening between two houses, keeping to the shadows. The palm fronds rustled in the breeze. Everything was so quiet and peaceful here. How could this be happening?

There was a car waiting. A black sedan. When they opened the door, no light came on. It had been fixed that way. He longed for a good look at the two men. All he could really tell was that they were tall and knew how to rough a man up if need be.

He was shoved into the back seat. Then quietly, the car was started and they purred through the streets. He thought of throwing himself out of the moving car. But the man in the front seat turned toward him, gun in his hand.

"Don't try anything. Understand?"

"Yeah," Bert nodded. "I've got you. Where are we going?"

"To a nice quiet spot we know. Where we can talk and you can tell us everything there is to tell about Juan Gonzales."

"I don't know any Juan Gonzales."

"Yeah, sure," the man said. "Never laid eyes on the man, did you?"

They were staying to the side streets. In the light of streetlamps, Bert tried for a good look. The man under the wheel had dark hair, a well-shaped head. But Bert couldn't get a look at his face. The other man, the pistol in his hand, was thin faced, had large, sinewy arms and hands, a broad forehead and thin lips.

At last the car was slowing down. Bert wasn't sure, but he thought he knew which area of town they were in. It was on the south outskirts. A little motel called the Flamingo. It wasn't well lighted and wasn't the best motel in Gull Haven by far. They drove around to the rear of the motel and there they stopped the car.

"Get out," he was told.

Bert nodded. It was now or never. Did he dare try? Who were these men? Which side of the fence were they on and how had they known about him?

Play it cool, he decided. Like in a poker game. Say nothing. Just take the cards as they were dealt.

They pushed open the door of number nine and

shoved him inside. Then the key turned in the lock behind him.

"Hey! Hey! Let me out of here," he shouted, pounding on the door.

Then a light came on in the room and he whirled about. In the brightness, he blinked. The man sitting in the chair also had a gun. He gave him a cool smile.

"Sit down. Let's have a long talk, shall we?"

Bert swallowed hard. He wasn't chicken. Normally, he flouted the devil when it came to taking risks, whether it be with a boat, a car, or a woman. But now, this was just a little different. Outside were two men, probably both armed. Inside, waiting patiently, was still another armed man.

"What do you want of me?" Bert asked. "What's this all about? Who are you?"

"My name's Monroe, Mr. Goodwin, and we want answers."

XIII

EVERYONE HAD LEFT the playhouse but Nollie, of course, and Lee wasn't exactly pleased with the way things were going.

"How're the ticket sales now, Nollie?" Lee asked.

Nollie had been totaling up the figures and shook his wiry, red head.

"Not so hot, Lee. If you don't draw any better crowds than this with first nights—what's it going to be later on?"

"Yeah," Lee sighed. "I know what you mean, Nollie. What we need is a gimmick. Something to sell tickets."

"Wait until they get a load of me!" Nollie said. "They'll come running."

Lee usually took Nollie's nonsensical boasting in stride, but tonight it irritated him.

"Oh, sure, Nollie. That's why you're such a great Hollywood star, in demand on TV and Broadway—"

Nollie blinked and for a moment, Lee thought he'd made him angry.

"Sorry, Nollie. I shouldn't have said that."

Nollie tossed his pencil aside. "Why not? I suppose it's true. But it's going to change one of these days, Lee. It sure is!"

"Well, when you find your fortune, let me know where and I'll look for mine."

Lee went into his living quarters and slammed the door behind him. Nothing was going quite right. Tonight's rehearsal had been very ragged. The first act of his new play didn't satisfy him. It didn't look as if the playhouse was going to get off to a very good start. With a sigh, he snapped on a light at the desk, picked up the pages of the first act and began to read. Then he was reaching for a pencil, making changes, adding lines, taking some out. When he finished at last, he saw by his watch that it was after two o'clock.

His head felt foggy. What he needed was some fresh air, maybe a sandwich from an all-night diner.

He went to knock on Nollie's door. "Hey, Nollie, wake up. Let's go out."

But Nollie didn't reply and there was no sound of his familiar snoring. Lee pushed open the door. The cot Nollie had been using was empty.

Nollie had gone out. It was like him. He kept crazy hours. Tonight, he'd left rehearsals early and when he'd chewed him out about it he'd gotten a little hot under the collar. Nollie was a funny guy. Outwardly a comic. Inwardly, a seething man who was angry with the world.

Lee gave up the idea of going to the diner. He didn't want to go alone. Instead, he settled for a stroll along the beach. It was different at night. He walked leisurely, trying to relax, to unknot the tangles his brain had been left in by his hard work on the play.

With a start, he saw someone ahead of him, coming his way. Who else would be out at such an hour?

"Nollie?" he wondered with surprise.

Nollie paused, as if stunned at the sight of him, then walked nonchalantly toward him.

"What's the matter, Lee? Couldn't you sleep?" Nollie asked.

"Just wanted to unwind. What are you doing out here? Were you over there by the old house?"

"Just roaming. Couldn't sleep. Beautiful night. Clear. Not a boat out there."

"There usually isn't, you know."

"Oh, I've seen several boats out late at night. Always wonder what they're doing, where they're going. Sometimes wish I was on board with them."

"Nollie, are you getting itchy feet again?" Lee asked. "You wouldn't walk out on me, right in the middle of things, would you?"

Nollie laughed. "Relax, man. I'm not going anywhere.

Not for a little while. Have to wait for my ship to come in, you know. Going back now?"

"Might as well," Lee sighed.

As they entered the playhouse, Lee paused for a moment, looking at the stage as it was revealed under the one light left burning there. He had such big dreams, such high ambitions. He had hoped the summer would be all he wanted it to be, but from all indications, it was starting out badly.

"Good night," Nollie called. "See you in the morning."

"Sure, Nollie," Lee nodded.

Lee was tired enough that he managed to fall asleep. The sea air often made him feel lazy.

It was late when he awakened. He smelled coffee. Nollie was making his usual witches' brew. Lee shook the sleep out of his eyes. It was another day. He'd have to see what he could do to make it count.

They had just finished breakfast when Angela Jones arrived.

"Hi, Lee," she said.

"Good morning, Angel. What brings you out so early?"

"Early?" she wrinkled her cute nose. "It's ten o'clock! There's still work to be done."

"So there is," Lee smiled. "Help yourself."

But Angel didn't move. She gave him a long look from under her silky lashes.

"Lee—"

"Hmm?"

"I—I was wondering. Would you like to drop by the house sometime? For dinner?"

It was the third time she had invited him and it was the third time he turned her down.

"Sorry, Angel. Just don't have the time for social amenities just now. Perhaps after we get rolling."

Angel reached out to touch his hand. "Okay, Lee. I'll wait."

Angel finally disappeared and he soon heard her talking with Nollie.

To his surprise, he had a second visitor. The man hesitated in the doorway, a tall man with black hair and gray eyes, dressed in casual clothes. Through the window, Lee caught sight of a low sports car. He'd seen him often walking on the beach.

"Hello," Lee said. "I'm Lee Tyler. Are you by any chance looking for me?"

"Yes," the man answered. "I'm Sutton Ward. I live just down the road. Larina Goodwin told you about me, I believe."

"Oh, yes. She certainly did and if you want to know if we can use you, the answer is yes."

Sutton Ward smiled slowly. "I haven't really made up my mind. I thought I'd just look around, see what's going on."

"I'll take you on the grand tour," Lee nodded. "This, of course, is the main auditorium. Our stage isn't big or fancy, but adequate. That racket you hear is a couple of my helpers."

"I understand you're going to write some of the plays yourself," Sutton said.

"Yes. I'm starting with one of my plays and I'm working on another. Then I have still one more that I think could be adapted to the playhouse. Otherwise, we'll stick to the tried and true stuff. We're going to be very ambitious. We're going to present a new play every week for about six weeks."

"I see," Sutton murmured.

Lee led him to the rear of the building. Angel was there, stitching a new cover on an old chair they planned to use in one of their sets. Nollie was hammering in another room.

"Oh, hello, Mr. Ward!" Angel said with surprise. "You don't know me, but I know you. I'm Angela Jones, but everyone around here calls me Angel."

Sutton nodded politely.

"Are you going to join us?" Angel asked with surprise, and it was plain to Lee that she liked the idea very much.

"Perhaps," Sutton replied cautiously. "I'm not sure I could be of any real help. Who's making all the racket?"

"That's my right-hand man, Nollie Oliver," Lee said. "I'd like you to meet him."

But the hammering had stopped and when Lee took Sutton into the workshop, Nollie was gone.

"That's funny. He was here just a second ago," Lee said with a frown.

Lee went back to the door and shouted. "Hey, Nollie, where are you?"

"I didn't see him leave," Angel said.

"He must have left by the window," Lee said with amusement. "That nut. You never know from one minute to the next what he'll do."

"This Mr. Oliver—is he a native of Gull Haven?"

Lee lifted his shoulders in a shrug. "No. I haven't the vaguest idea where he really comes from. He just drifted in here and wanted a job. I'll have to admit he knows his way around a theatre."

"I'm disappointed that I didn't get to meet him," Sutton said easily. "He sounds interesting."

"Interesting," Lee nodded. "If you don't mind hearing a lot of wild talk and a little name-dropping. But Nollie's okay. He's been a big help to me. Well, Mr. Ward, that's about it. We're in rehearsal for our first play and our first performance is set for next weekend. I'm not at all sure we'll be ready, but the show will go on—one way or another."

"Well, perhaps I'll wait until you start a new play. Then, maybe, but no promises," Sutton said.

"We'd be happy to have you," Lee said.

"Thank you."

Sutton shook Lee's hand and said a quick good-bye. Lee frowned. What had he really come for? He had a queer feeling that Sutton hadn't really heard a word he'd said. Lee doubted very much if the man would be back.

Lee spent the morning with his play, the afternoon helping Angel with the props and by evening, he was tired and keyed up, with rehearsals still facing him. Nollie had come back to the playhouse about noon and when Lee questioned him, he shrugged his shoulders.

"Had a little business, that's all."

"How did you get out of here so quick?"

The Season of Love

"I just walked out. Guess you didn't see me. Or Angel either. What's wrong?"

"Nothing," Lee said. "You just have a peculiar way about you sometimes, Nollie."

Nollie grinned. "I'm just an original. That's all."

There were a couple of hours yet before rehearsal time and Lee decided to drive into town and pay a visit to Tish Morgan. Tish was a good scout and level-headed. She was also Larina's best friend in Gull Haven.

The town was still busy but Lee was lucky enough to find a parking place. Then, walking briskly down the street, he pushed open the door to Tish's shop. Tish was busy with a customer, but waggled a couple of fingers at him and motioned for him to wait.

When she had finished at last, she went to lock the door. Store hours were over.

"Hello, Lee. This is a nice surprise. What ever rooted you away from the playhouse?"

He smiled at that. "A chance to take you to supper. Okay?"

"Why not? How're things going out there?"

Lee shook his head, unable to hide his discouragement. "Not so hot, Tish. If we're really ready to put on our first performance Thursday night, I'll be surprised."

"We'll make it," Tish said. "It's a mess now, but it will straighten out."

"But what will we be playing to, a handful of people?" Lee asked miserably. "The ticket sales aren't moving at all."

"Maybe some more ads—"

"I had Larina paint some extra posters and Nollie's got them all over town."

"I think you need a good, hot supper," Tish said with a shake of her blonde head. "That will make you feel better."

They selected a little cafe near Tish's shop, where they ordered the day's special which Tish vowed would be good. Lee was frankly a little tired of his own cooking.

"Anyone show up to help today?" Tish asked.

"Angel was there early and then a couple of others this afternoon. But that's all."

"Angel?" Tish asked slyly.

Lee met Tish's mischievous eyes.

"Now, Tish—"

"Look, anybody can tell the girl's sweet on you."

Lee fingered his coffee cup. "Oh, Angel's a good kid. Works hard. Doesn't do too badly on the stage. But—"

"But there's Larina Goodwin. Right?"

Lee nodded. "Yes. Tish, you're a good friend, aren't you? I mean of Larina's?"

"Yes. You know I am."

"Can you give me a clue or two? I mean, about what's happened to her. I know something has."

Tish shook her head. "I'm sorry, Lee, I really don't know myself. She hasn't wanted to talk about it. I can only assume that something has happened—I mean—unhappily—"

"You think she's broken off with some guy?" Lee asked hopefully.

Tish nodded. "That's my guess. Or they had a big fight. One or the other. Oh, Larina seems the same. Outgoing and warm. That's the way she's made. But once in a while, she seems so far away, so sad."

"She's a lovely girl," Lee said softly. "I—I suppose I made a terrible blunder."

"How?"

Lee remembered that day on the beach, when he had proposed they have a summer affair. He had implied that it wouldn't necessarily be a serious or lasting thing, just a pleasant pastime for the long, hot summer. But he felt afterward that he had offended her. Larina simply wasn't the sort that went in for that sort of thing. He should have known that.

"Well, tell me!" Tish said with exasperation.

So he explained and Tish listened, a look of horror on her face.

"You didn't!"

"Yes," Lee said miserably. "I did. I wish I could take back every word I said."

"I should think so!"

"The funny part of it is, Tish, I don't think I feel that way anymore. I mean, I think—"

"You want it to be serious?"

Lee nodded. "Yes. I'm a little surprised at myself. But I like Larina quite a lot. In fact, I think I've fallen in love with her."

Tish waited a moment before saying anything. Then with a wry smile, she lifted her coffee cup to her lips.

"Why are you telling me all this, Lee? I'm the wrong girl. Tell Larina."

Lee nodded. "Yes," he smiled. "I think I will! The very first chance I get."

XIV

LARINA HAD PUT her studio in order. Her materials were laid out neatly, she had selected a large canvas and had it squarely on her easel. The draperies had been pulled open wide to let in all the brilliant sunlight that Florida had to offer. She had spent the entire morning getting ready, discarding one idea after another, until finally she had decided how she wanted to pose Sutton Ward.

He was due at eleven o'clock and Bertha had promised to bring them lunch on a tray. They would make a long session of it and she wanted to start off with him relaxed. So many subjects froze in front of a camera or an artist's analytical eyes.

She was more than a little excited about painting Sutton. Especially after their outing to Tarpon Springs and what had happened that day.

The breeze came in off the Gulf and stirred the draperies. A sailboat went skimming by her window and she took time to watch it. Was there anything else as graceful or as lovely on the water as that?

Then she heard Sutton's steps and his knock at the door. She went to let him in.

"Hello, Sutton."

"Am I late?"

"No."

"I visited the playhouse for a little while," he said. "I met Mr. Tyler."

"Oh? Didn't you think it was exciting what they were doing? So much imagination, so much talent, so much of everything!"

Sutton laughed. He leaned toward her and kissed her lips for a warm moment.

"Yes. I suppose so. Would you think I was backward or something if I said I didn't really get that excited?"

"No. Of course not. Not everyone's interested in theatre work."

"Larina, about this portrait—"

He was nervous about it. His eyes wandered about the snug little studio.

"Say, this is nice."

"Uncle Ernie fixed it for me. He must have moved heaven and earth to get it ready on such short notice. But Uncle Ernie's like that."

"Where do I sit?"

"Over there. By the windows."

"Larina, I'm not sure about this. Not at all."

She laughed. "Oh, relax, Sutton. It won't hurt a bit."

She posed him in the chair as she wanted and stood back for a long, hard look. He flushed at her stare.

Then picking up her charcoal, she began making a preliminary sketch, working swiftly, surely.

"I'll have to ask you to sit as still as possible. At least for a little while."

"All right," Sutton nodded. "You can look at me, but you know something, Larina? I can look right back at you!"

Their glances met and locked for one pulsing moment, and she remembered the time in his car when he had kissed her so warmly and she had kissed him back. Oh, what had gotten into her? What had she meant by doing that? She was in love with John, wasn't she? She had certainly thought so when she came down here to Florida for the summer.

But there had not been any letter. Dad had written her a couple of times, but there was no mail from John. Had he so completely forgotten her?

"I want you to be free this summer," he'd told her. "Just as I want to be free."

She blinked fast. Now was not the time to think about John. Now was the time to concentrate on the sketch she was making, on the handsome, dark face of the man sitting in the chair by the window.

She worked for an hour and put down her charcoal when she heard Bertha's steps outside her door.

Bertha came in with a large tray. Sutton leaped to his feet to take it from her hands.

"Thank you, Bertha."

"How are you, Mr. Ward?" Bertha asked.

"At the moment, not too comfortable," Sutton said with his slow but charming smile. "Did you ever sit for a portrait, Bertha?"

Bertha laughed. "Never!"

The food on the tray looked appetizing and refreshing for such a warm day. Larina set it out on a small table which Sutton moved to the windows and there, they sat down to lunch.

"Hmm. You have no idea how much I appreciate this," Sutton said with a grin. "Bertha's a great cook."

"You know what I think?" Larina asked. "I think this is the only reason you agreed to sit for me. You wouldn't promise until I told you I'd give you lunch."

Sutton stretched out a hand to take hers. "Darling, I'll admit the lunch was tempting, but there's something much more tempting in this room."

"Oh, Sutton, you shouldn't say things like that."

"Why not? When I mean them?"

"Concentrate on your sandwiches. Please."

Sutton laughed. "Oh, I hope it takes a month of Sundays for you to do my portrait."

The lunch was tasty, the company was good, and the weather was perfect, although for the last couple of days, there had been a hazy look on the horizon. A thunder storm was building up, just hanging out there, waiting to move in. But she rather liked the beach in the rain. Everything seemed one color then. The gray rain, the gray-green churning ocean and even the sand seemed gray as it was soaked with a summer shower. She always wondered where all the birds went when it rained. All those gulls and sandpipers and pelicans.

"You're enjoying your summer here, aren't you?" Sutton asked.

She nodded. "Yes. More than I thought I would."

"I hope I had a little to do with you changing your mind."

"Perhaps," she nodded.

"And Lee Tyler?"

She laughed. "How did he get into this conversation?"

"You have been up there a great deal of the time. I saw you one day, having a picnic lunch on the beach with him."

"You did?"

"Yes."

"Keeping tabs on me?" she wondered with a tiny little frown.

"Not really."

"I'm the sort that makes friends easily, Sutton. But you aren't, are you?"

He took another bite of Bertha's delicious potato salad and shook his head.

"No. I suppose not, really. I do get around a great deal. I know a lot of people. But for really good friends, I don't suppose I have a great many."

"What a shame! I think the world would be an awful place without friends."

"Maybe I'm more of a loner," he said. "I'm glad you have friends, Larina. It must be lonely here with just your aunt for company."

"I'm hoping Uncle Ernie will come home for a weekend. He's always so much fun."

"Don't they have any children?"

"Yes. A son. Bert. But he's away."

"Oh?" Sutton asked casually. "Vacation?"

"Bert's on a perpetual vacation. He's a little like you, Sutton."

"In what way?"

"Travels a great deal. Thrives on new places, new people. He jets here and there. You never know where he'll be."

"And where is he now?" Sutton asked.

Larina looked at him. Her heart did an unreasonable dance inside her chest. She wasn't one to lie. But what else could she do? She'd done nothing but worry about

Bert ever since he'd shown up beneath her window, bewhiskered and obviously in trouble.

"The last we knew, he was going to Mexico," she said quickly. "Why do you ask?"

Sutton shrugged. "Just like to meet him, that's all. Sounds like we have a great deal in common."

"Yes," Larina said.

Nervously, she poured them another glass of lemonade. She wondered if Sutton might have seen Bert slipping around the house! But if he had, surely he would mention it. How could he know who Bert was? Anyone would have taken him for a prowler.

"They think the drug smugglers are operating out of Mexico. Did you know that?" Sutton asked.

"Yes. I heard it on the news."

"I was at the country club the other day. Everyone seems to think that a really big deal is cooking."

"Big deal?" Larina asked with a wrinkled nose. "What do you mean?"

"The smugglers. I don't know how these people got their information, but they thought a very large shipment of drugs was to reach the Florida coast, somewhere in this vicinity this week."

"How could anyone possibly know a thing like that?"

Sutton shook his head with a smile. "I don't know. Everyone's just guessing, I imagine. Is that chocolate cake I see peeking out from under that napkin?"

"My very favorite," Larina explained. "Bertha bakes it for me. I love it!"

"I'll try a piece."

The lunch was a long one. Neither was in a hurry for it to end. They talked of many things. Larina was glad when Sutton left the subject of the smugglers. She didn't want to think about it. Nor did she want to think about Bert and what trouble he could be in. He had been in Mexico. She knew that. Now Sutton was telling her the drug smugglers were working out of there. There couldn't be any connection, could there?

When they went back to work at last, the sun was beginning to grow hazy. The clouds were rolling in at last and if Larina didn't miss her guess, it would be raining within an hour. She worked until the light began to go. Then, wiping her brushes clean, she told Sutton he could relax.

"Through for the day?" he asked.

"Yes."

"Was that thunder?"

"Yes," Larina said. "We're in for a downpour."

"Do you want me to go now?"

Larina very busily put her brushes aside. Sutton was waiting for an answer.

"It's going to pour," she said. "You know how it rains here. In torrents."

"I'd like to stay."

Then he was crossing the room to her and his arms went around her. "Don't make me go, Larina."

"Oh, Sutton, what am I going to do with you? What am I going to do about myself?"

"Tell me about yourself. I'd like to hear. Let's sit there by the windows and you tell me about Larina Goodwin, from the time you were a little girl until now."

"It would be boring."

"It could never be boring," Sutton told her.

He pulled up the small sofa and they sat there, close together, Sutton's arm around her, and he questioned her, drawing her out, until she found herself telling him everything about herself. She even dared to mention John.

"John?" he asked. "He's special, isn't he?"

"Yes. We teach in the same school. John is warm and lively and exciting—"

"I see," Sutton said slowly. "And what happened between you?"

She didn't want to think about it or talk about it, but to her surprise, she did. Sutton watched her closely, his gray eyes flickering.

"He said you were to be free, is that right?"

She nodded. Then Sutton reached out and cupped her face in his hands. She was aware of the softness about his lips, the tenderness in his eyes. She had never seen Sutton like this. Always, he seemed to be partially on guard, as if he were forever listening for an unexpected footstep. But now, this minute, there was no one else in the world but them.

"I love you, Larina. I don't mind telling you, it complicates things, but I love you."

"What things?"

"I can't tell you now. Sometime—soon, I will."

"You're being very mysterious."

"I'm sorry."

She pulled out of his arms. In a moment, she was going to forget who she was, forget John even existed.

"What is it, Larina?"

"I don't know you, Sutton. I know nothing about you except that you have a bad back, live in a very large, expensive house, drive a sports car, and are frequently gone for unexplained lengths of time. I just don't know what to make of you."

He stared at her for a moment. He clamped his lips shut. His fists knotted and unknotted.

"Larina, I love you. I want you to love me. And if you do fall in love with me, can't you accept me on blind faith? Isn't that what love's all about?"

"Why must I accept you on blind faith? Why can't you tell me about yourself, Sutton? What are you hiding?"

He got to his feet. Outside, the rain came down in driving sheets. They were forced to close the windows. Sutton paced restlessly. Once, he seemed about to say something and then changed his mind.

He came at last to put his arms around her again.

"I was born in New York State. I went to college there. I was going to be a lawyer, but I dropped out of law school. I inherited a lot of dough. I—I decided to see the world. To find out what made it tick. I've had a good time, I won't deny that. Is that so wrong?"

"You're like Bert," she said tiredly. "Exactly like Bert!"

Sutton laughed. "But you like your cousin. In fact, I think you probably adore him. Why not me too?"

Then he wasn't waiting for any answer. He was kissing

her, very soundly. When he let her go at last, she had lost all her arguments, all her reason, all her good sense.

What was happening to her? Was she falling in love with a rich playboy, a man of the world whom she hardly knew? Could it happen like that to her?

XV

Sutton left the studio late that afternoon, long after the rain had stopped.

"Shall I come back tomorrow?" he asked.

"Yes. I'd like to stay with this until it's done."

"Good," he said with a smile that was both teasing and serious.

Then with one sweep of his arms, he pulled her close.

"Ah, Larina, you're quite a girl."

"Am I?" she asked.

"Yes. To me, you're very special."

She managed a laugh and tilted her head in a provocative way. "I bet you've told women that from one end of the world to the other."

"No," he shook his head. "I'm not a man that uses words that way. Remember that, Larina."

Then he was gone and she stood for a long while, remembering the day, the long session at her easel, the changing moods that she had caught from time to time across his face. There were moments when he seemed far away, when a little line cut into his forehead between his eyes and she knew that he was concentrating hard on something. Once, she had asked him about it but he had simply shaken his head, straightened his shoulders and smiled. There was something very deep about Sutton Ward. There was more to the man than met the eye.

She looked at the work she'd done and was pleased. Sutton was a good subject. She hadn't been wrong about that. Putting things into good order again, she went out into the rain-washed air. The sky was turning blue again and the sand was already beginning to dry.

"Larina!"

Aunt Stella was calling to her. She called back and hurried toward the house.

"My, I thought you'd never finish. Did you paint that man's picture all that time?"

Larina laughed. "No. Not all the time. When the rain came, the light wasn't good enough, so I quit."

"Larina, I'm not one to poke my nose in your affairs, but do you think you'd ought to be seeing quite so much of Sutton Ward?"

The question surprised her. She laughed. "Of course! He's not going to bite, Aunt Stell. He's really very nice."

"Just one little word of warning and then I'll not say anything more," Aunt Stell said. "I don't want you to be hurt. Sutton seems to be quite a man about town. There's gossip that he gambles. What else can explain the way strange men come and go from his house?"

"You don't want me to see him again, is that it?" Larina asked.

"Goodness, Larina, I can't tell you who to see and who not to see! I just want you to be forewarned."

"All right. Consider it done," Larina nodded. "Thank you, Aunt Stell."

Aunt Stell sighed and rubbed the fingers where they extended from the heavy cast on her wrist. "I had to say it. I know Ernie would have wanted me to."

"How is your wrist?" Larina asked.

"Itching. Knitting, I suppose. But it's about to drive me wild. That and a few other things."

"Your committee meetings haven't been going very well, have they?"

Aunt Stella sighed. "No. They certainly haven't."

"Aunt Stell, I'd like to bring Jimmy here, for a picnic and a romp on the beach. Would that be all right?"

"Of course! You know it would. I'm sure they'll give you permission."

"I'll try to do it soon. Very soon. I think I'll take a walk on the beach. Want to join me?"

Aunt Stell shook her head. "Not this time. Thanks anyway."

So Larina went alone. She thought about Aunt Stell

and her committees. They were trying to be helpful. But how could they raise the needed money for Calley's Home? Well, if she could just get a brainstorm . . .

Her thoughts strayed to Sutton. He had asked about Bert. It had surprised her. Did Sutton know Bert? No. Surely not. But he had probably heard about him. Bert was well known in Gull Haven.

She paused for a moment to stare out to the water, thinking. Where was Bert? What was he doing? Would he come again? What kind of trouble had brought him home in such dire circumstances? For half a cent, she would tell Aunt Stell about his visit. But how could she betray Bert's confidence?

That evening, after a light supper, she borrowed the convertible. The one place Bert might be, she decided, was the Peterson Orange Grove. It wouldn't hurt to drive out there and look around. As kids, they had haunted the place and Bert, like herself, knew all the buildings, the packing sheds, the garage, even the house. The Petersons were nice, open-hearted people and oddly enough, Peterson and Bert had always been friends. Still, there were not two men anywhere who were so completely different.

Larina enjoyed the drive through the streets of Gull Haven. She felt relaxed and almost happy tonight. Was that the influence of a day spent in Sutton's company?

"What's the matter with me?" she wondered. "I'm like a high school girl with her first crush."

She laughed at that. Then humming as she drove, she pushed the car down the highway, leaving Gull Haven behind. In a few minutes, she had reached the grove. She turned in at the sandy drive and went along the rows and rows of orange trees. Then, stopping at last, she left the car and walked into the grove toward a small shed. It was just dusk and if anyone saw her, they would wonder what on earth she was doing. With a laugh, she knew she must look like some kind of sneak thief.

"Bert!" she called. "Bert! Are you there?"

She pushed open the door. Stepping inside, she looked around in the murky semidarkness. But there was only an assortment of tools and various equipment that Peterson used.

"Bert—"

She felt a sharp ache of disappointment. She had been hoping to find her cousin here. Where else would he be? It was impossible to know and she was certain any searching on her part would be futile. This had been her only hope.

With a sigh, she left the shed and walked back to her car. Driving on, she reached an open fruit-stand that Peterson operated. He was a big, rawboned Swede and when he saw her, he wrung her hand with delight.

"Hello, Larina! Didn't know you were paying us a visit."

"Yes, for the summer."

"What can I sell you tonight?"

She made a couple of small purchases, talking lightly, laughing at old jokes as Peterson remembered the way she and Bert used to haunt the place.

"How is that old rascal?" Peterson asked. "Haven't seen him in months!"

Her hopes took a dive. "He's in Mexico, I think," she managed to answer. "Who knows!"

"That's for sure. Bert never let any grass grow under his feet."

She lingered for a few moments of small talk, then waved good-bye and drove away. So, Peterson hadn't seen him. Where was he hiding? How could she find him?

She was more than a little worried about him. For one thing, he had no money, and what little she'd given him wouldn't last long. His trouble must be serious, very serious, for him to have acted as he had.

It was still early and she didn't want to go home. So she drove to the playhouse. They were nearing their first performance and as she slipped into the theatre, she took a chair in the rear of the building.

"No, no, no!" Lee was shouting abruptly, leaping up to the stage. "Not like that, Angel. Feeling. Put feeling into it! This is a man with flesh and blood you're talking to, not a bundle of sticks!"

"I'm trying," Angel said in a hurt voice. "I'm trying! Please, don't shout at me!"

"I *have* to shout! Can't you understand that we're about to perform before a live audience and you're not ready?"

Angel burst into tears at that and rushed off the stage. Lee threw his hands in the air.

"Okay, everybody. Take a break. Fifteen minutes. Somebody talk to Angel."

Lee looked tired. He ran a hand through his brown hair. Larina felt sorry for him. He had worked so terribly, terribly hard. Everyone was on edge. Time was getting away and nothing was going right. Larina knew the feeling.

She walked down the aisle to the stage. Lee heard her steps and looked around with surprise.

"Larina!"

"Why don't we take a walk, get some air?" she asked with a smile. "I think you need it."

Lee laughed awkwardly. "You can say that again."

He tossed the script aside and, taking her arm, walked swiftly to the door and stepped outside with her. It was cooler tonight after the rain.

"I'm beginning to wonder if the play will ever come off. Maybe I'm just wasting my summer here. Maybe I should just pack up and go home, finish my play there."

"You're only discouraged," Larina said. "Tomorrow, it will be much better. Wait and see."

He took her hand as they stepped down into the deep, white sand and began walking toward the old Bleaker house.

"The ticket sales are disappointing. We're not even going to meet expenses. Wave your magic wand, will you?" he asked. "Make a miracle."

"Oh, I wish I could, Lee. I really do!"

He stopped walking then and tugged her toward him. She tried to hold him off, but he wasn't to be held. He kissed her forehead lightly.

"What's wrong?"

"Haven't you enough on your mind?" she asked in a teasing voice.

"When I looked around and saw you, it was the highlight of my day."

"Lee, please, don't ruin our friendship!"

"I wasn't trying to," he told her. "Don't you understand, Larina—"

She walked on. She didn't want to hear. Things were coming much too fast.

"Larina—" He came after her. "Larina—"

"Lee, I think we'd better get back to the theatre. The fifteen minutes will be up and everyone will be waiting for you."

He nodded slowly. "All right, Larina. But soon, very soon, I want to have a serious talk with you."

Everyone was waiting for Lee. He gave the signal and everyone took his place on the stage again. Angel Jones had dried her tears, and with hard determination she tackled her role. Lee made her go over her lines two more times and then he seemed satisfied.

Nollie came to sit down beside Larina.

"Hi."

"Hello, Nollie."

"I'll have to say this for Lee. He's a perfectionist."

"Nollie, I think the play's good. Really good. But Lee's so depressed."

"I know."

"Is it that bad, really?"

Nollie hunched his shoulders in a good-natured shrug.

"Probably not. We just need a good box office. You know, Larina, cold cash eases a lot of headaches."

"I know," she said wearily, thinking of Aunt Stell and her committee.

Nollie rubbed a hand over his crew cut red hair. "Well, one of these days, I'll be in the chips."

She paid little attention to Nollie. Nollie was a braggart, a lovable braggart perhaps, but still a braggart.

Larina watched a few more minutes of the rehearsal and decided to leave. After a time, it got a little boring. Driving home, she thought again of Bert. Every night, she expected him to come again and he didn't. What had happened to him, where had he gone?

Worry nagged at her and as she drove in the garage

at home and put down the door, she looked around at the shadows. If only he'd step out and show himself. If only she could talk to him again! The next time, she wouldn't let him get away without giving her some answers.

Aunt Stell had retired to her room on the ground floor and Larina looked in for a moment as she went to her own.

"I'm home," she called.

Aunt Stell looked up with a smile. "So, I see. Have a nice time?"

"I watched the rehearsals again. They aren't going well and everything up there is in sort of a mess."

"Like our charity drive," Aunt Stell said sympathetically.

They chatted a few minutes longer and then Larina called good night. She was halfway up the stairs when the idea hit her.

"Aunt Stell! Aunt Stell!" she ran back.

"My goodness, what *is* it? What's wrong?"

"I've got a marvelous idea that will help you and Lee too! I'm sure Lee would go along with it."

Aunt Stell shook her head with exasperation. "My goodness, what's got into you?"

"You need to raise money. So does Lee. I'm sure Lee would sell a block of tickets a little cheaper just to sell them. You could then resell them at a higher price. You could do your bit for charity and yet give the donors something in return."

"Wait a minute, Larina—"

"Don't you see? Lee can give a performance at the playhouse to the holders of the charity tickets!"

Aunt Stell stared at her for a moment and then she began to smile.

"Why, Larina, that's an excellent idea."

"You'll be helping the Home, and Lee will be happy to have a crowd in the theatre. Of course! It's a perfect solution."

"I'll do it!" Aunt Stell said. "I'll see that young man tomorrow and see what we can work out."

They talked for a few more excited moments and then

at last Larina went to her room. Lee would be so pleased, she was sure.

With a sigh, she thought about him. Then Sutton came into her mind like a warm, sweet song and her face flushed. Why was she thinking so much about him? When everything about him was in shadow? Why did he seem to be hiding something?

XVI

SUTTON SPENT THE NEXT DAY in Larina's studio. While it was hard to sit so still for such long periods of time, he didn't want to complain. He had come to love the studio, with the sound of the surf outside the window, the blue sky as clear as an undisturbed mountain pool, and the sea quiet, almost placid.

He had a feeling of something building up, of an explosion all set to start from a sputtering fuse. But that was still in the future. Today, things were breathing easily. Everyone and everything seemed relaxed.

Larina was bubbling over with plans for a benefit drive to sell tickets to a playhouse production. He scarcely followed what she was saying. Most of it seemed to be mixed up with a little boy called Jimmy.

"Should I be jealous?" he asked.

"Of Jimmy? Oh, Sutton, he's a marvelous little boy. So sweet. So sad. My heart just breaks for him—"

"Hey, I *am* getting jealous!"

She laughed at that and went back to her painting. He agreed to buy at least ten tickets to help the charity drive and that small gesture delighted her.

He loved watching her face as she worked. At times she was completely absorbed with a little line of concentration in her forehead. Then other times she looked at him with dreams in her eyes and she relaxed, her voice lilting as she talked. She was unspoiled. Somehow, the world had not really touched her and it was this that he loved so much. For he had seen much of the world, not always the good side, too often the worst.

"Sutton—"

"Yes?"

"Would you lift your chin, just a little? Thank you."

He felt a little idiotic posing for her. But what better way to spend the daytime hours? He had left word where he could be reached, but he hoped he never received a phone call here. For one thing, it might be hard to explain. For another, he guarded these hours with Larina with all his energy.

"How's your back?"

She fussed like a little mother hen over him, always inquiring about his back, making sure that he took a rest break every few minutes, pounding him with questions, some of which he had to sidestep.

"I'm all right, Larina," he said now. "But thank you for asking."

She put her brush down, stood back, and cocked her head first one way and then another as she looked at her work.

"Well, how is it?" he asked with amusement.

"Handsome," she laughed. "You're a very handsome man, Sutton Ward."

He flushed at that.

"Come over here and say that," he challenged.

She shook her head with a laugh. "I want to finish and if I go over there, I won't."

She picked up her brush again. Another five minutes of silence and he began to stir. He heard Bertha's steps outside the door.

Larina went to let her in. Bertha gave him a quick, hard glance. Bertha did not approve of him. For that matter, he doubted if Stella Goodwin did either. Luckily, Ernie was still in Europe. The two women he could handle. But Ernie Goodwin—it was doubtful.

"Ah, Bertha, what ambrosia have you brought us today?" Sutton asked, getting to his feet and going over to peer at the tray.

"Just what Larina ordered," Bertha said stiffly.

"You're about the best cook I know, Bertha," he said easily.

Bertha hesitated. She wanted to respond, but she

didn't like him and she didn't trust him. Sutton laughed. Bertha disappeared with a flip of her white apron.

"Bertha doesn't know what to make of you, Sutton," Larina said.

"I know," he grinned.

"Why do you tease her?"

"I suppose I want her to like me," he said. "As much as I want you to love me."

Larina moved away to the window, keeping her back to him. She didn't know what to do when he said things like that. He could sense that the girl was torn. Did he dare hope that she was falling in love with him?

"Larina—"

He put his arms around her and pulled her back against him. Like that, they gazed for a long time at the sea and then he couldn't bear it any longer. With a swift motion, he turned her to face him and he began kissing her, as if drunk with her nearness.

"Ah, Larina, Larina, Larina—"

He could sense that she was weakening. Each time he kissed her, he was more and more sure of it. But when would she finally give in? When would the final little break come? Soon! Let it be soon! Before those lights began blinking out on the sea, before the signal was returned, before he was forced to become involved.

"Sutton, you mustn't do that!" she scolded. "You simply overwhelm me. It—it isn't fair."

He laughed at that and took her face in his hands.

"Darling, all's fair in love and war."

He let her go at last. Then they shared lunch, and for a lonely man, it was a treat just to have a pretty girl across the table from him. But when it was Larina, it was more than just a treat.

A little spasm of pain chased across his back and for a moment he stopped eating, willing it to go away. But it was always there, a constant reminder of who he was and what he had to do. With one hand, he reached back and massaged it, feeling the little welts of scars beneath his fingers.

"Did you bring your capsules?" Larina asked.

"Yes. In my coat pocket."

"I'll get them," she said.

Before he could leap to his feet and stop her, she had gone over to the chair where he'd hung his coat. He'd been posing for her in shirt sleeves. Now, she was thrusting her hands into his pockets and he was conscious of terror rippling along his nerves.

"The outside pocket," he said. "On the left—"

But for some reason, she had dipped her small hand into the inner breast-pocket. A strange, half-frightened look came over her face.

"Sutton—"

"The outside pocket," he said desperately.

But it was too late. She'd found the gun. With two fingers she pulled it out of the pocket, a look of horror on her face. She nearly dropped it. Then he limped to her side and took it away from her.

"You—you carry a gun?" she gasped.

"A hangover from my Monte Carlo days," he said quickly. "I—I used to handle large sums of money."

"As a gambler," she said tonelessly.

He didn't know where she got that idea but he did nothing to change it. Obviously, there had been a great deal of speculation about him in Gull Haven and she'd heard some of it.

"A gun!" she shuddered, repulsed.

He decided to treat it casually.

"It's all right, Larina. It doesn't mean a thing. I'll—I'll get rid of it. Put it away."

"But you always carry it, don't you? I remember that first day I knew about your back, I helped you to the house. Remember?"

"Of course!" he said sharply. "Of course, I remember!"

"I went to find your capsules. I remember there was something hard and heavy swinging in that inside pocket. Now, I know it was a gun!"

She was aghast at the idea. He laughed and went to put his hands on her shoulders.

"Darling, a lot of men carry guns. I wouldn't be surprised that if your uncle ever carries large sums for the bank, that he carries one too."

"No. Not ever!"

"Just because I have a gun doesn't mean—"

He broke off. What could he say? The more he talked, the less she seemed to believe him. She was staring at him with round, gray-blue eyes, as if she was suddenly seeing him for the first time. He swore under his breath. Why hadn't he left it home? But he couldn't. Not until this business in Florida was settled. He never knew when he might need it. Rubbing a hand across the scars on his back, he knew that he would never risk leaving it behind.

"Why do you carry it, Sutton? I want the truth."

He took a deep breath. "Darling, you'll have to trust me. You'll have to bear with me. Just for a little while longer. Then—then I'll tell you everything."

She shook her head. "No. Now."

"I can't!" he said angrily. "Don't you understand? I can't."

"No, Sutton, I don't understand. Call me stupid or whatever you want, but I don't understand!"

He shouldn't have let himself get involved. Not at such a crucial time. But it was something he couldn't seem to control. All his willpower and good sense seemed to desert him when he was with this girl.

"You'll have to trust me, Larina. I can't say anything more."

"I have to know what's going on!" she said. "I have to know, Sutton."

He looked at her for a moment. Her cheeks were pink and her eyes were now sea-green. They were always like that when she was angry. With a sigh, he knew it was useless to stay any longer. The mood was shattered. If he stayed, he might be tempted to tell her and he couldn't risk that.

"I'm sorry, Larina. I'm very sorry."

Then he picked up his jacket and walked to the door. Larina stood at the window keeping her back to him. With a sigh, he called good-bye.

He walked briskly across the patio and then through the sand to the Bardwell house. He both loved and loathed the place. He loved it because it had brought him into Larina's life and he loathed it because of why he was here in the first place.

Going inside he paced about for a little while, thinking. Everything was quiet. Perhaps too quiet. He reached for the phone and dialed a number.

"Put Monroe on," he said.

He waited impatiently. Then Monroe's deep voice rumbled over the line.

"Got anything?" he asked.

"No. Nothing. He's like a clam."

"I'm coming out," Sutton said.

"You think that's smart?"

"I'm coming."

He hung up with a slam of the receiver. Monroe was a good man, a little nervous maybe, but generally, he knew his business. Sutton changed clothes, dressed as if going fishing, took his tackle along as a blind and got in his car. As he drove by the Goodwin place, he looked for a glimpse of Larina, but he couldn't see her anywhere.

Poor Larina. What must she be thinking? But he was powerless to do otherwise. Until the caper was over, he had to sit tight. Then when he was free of it at last—it might be a different story.

He drove quickly through the Gull Haven streets, left his car parked on a shady boulevard and hailed a cab. Then he had the cabdriver let him out two blocks from the motel. Even then he took extra precautions as he walked to the motel. Hiding behind sunglasses, he looked like any average man hustling about his business.

At last he stood before number nine. He rapped hard three times, followed by two swift knocks. The door was opened a crack and Monroe's beady eyes peered out at him.

"Let me in," Sutton said. "Be quick about it."

The chain was released and Sutton stepped inside. The curtains had been drawn and the room was shadowy. After the bright sunlight, he had to blink to see.

"Who are you?" a voice demanded.

The man in the chair had a black beard, a tall, slender frame, and a pair of frank, blue eyes.

"A friend," Sutton replied.

"Yeah. You're all friends. Real good buddies. Now look, fun's fun, but I'm getting a little tired of your merry-go-round. When do I get out of this dump?"

"When you cooperate," Sutton replied smoothly.

"Who are you? The boss?"

Sutton smiled coldly. "No. I'm not the boss. Just an interested party."

The blue eyes were studying him from head to toe. This man was no fool.

"We just want to know what you know about Juan Gonzales," Sutton said.

"For the hundredth time, I don't know any Juan Gonzales!"

"Come, come," Sutton said with a bored voice. "You don't really expect us to believe that, do you?"

"What's it to you?"

Sutton moved about the room, mindful of his back. He waited several seconds, saying nothing. Monroe slouched in a chair and put his feet up on the bed. Empty soda bottles littered the place, and Monroe was a chain smoker. The room was stale and untidy. Sutton wished he had stayed by the sea. It was doubtful he could do any more with this man than Monroe.

"You guys are going to be sorry when I get out of here, you're all going to prison! For kidnapping!"

Sutton laughed. "Are we?"

"You've got no right to hold me like this!"

Sutton sat down on the lumpy bed.

"Just give us a few straight answers and you can go. Number one, why were you in the Bleaker house?"

"Sight-seeing!"

"Why are you passing yourself off incognito?"

"Didn't you ever want to forget who you were?" came the cocky answer.

"In Mexico, you had dealings with Juan Gonzales. Now tell us about that."

"I had no dealings with Juan Gonzales."

"No," Sutton shook his head. "I suppose you didn't. It was more that he had dealings with you. Your disguise is good, but not that good. We know who you are."

"Yeah, I know that you know!"

"You refuse to cooperate?"

"Yes!"

"All right," Sutton said smoothly. "I guess you leave us no alternative, Mr. Goodwin. I believe you're quite fond of your cousin, Larina."

The man sat up as if a thunderbolt had struck him. His face went white beneath his beard.

"Don't you touch a hair of her head!" Goodwin yelled angrily. "Do you hear?"

Sutton nodded. "Oh, we hear all right, Bert. But the question is, do you hear us? Shall we try again? What dealings did Juan Gonzales have with you in Mexico?"

XVII

AUNT STELL INVITED Lee Tyler to the house for midmorning coffee the very next day and he was pleased with the invitation. Larina went to meet him when the old car pulled into their drive.

In the sun, Lee's brown hair looked burnished and his hazel eyes were quick and alert.

"Hello," Larina said. "We're so happy you could come."

Lee smiled. "Your aunt was quite insistent."

"I hope it isn't an inconvenience."

"I've more things to do than I can shake a stick at, but I couldn't pass up coffee with you and your aunt for anything," he told her.

Linking her arm through his, Larina led him into the house and through it to the patio. There, Bertha was just putting out the cups. Aunt Stella was there, looking a little tired. Larina suspected her wrist was bothering her more than she admitted.

"Aunt Stell, this is Lee Tyler. Lee, my aunt."

"I'm so happy to know you, Mr. Tyler," Aunt Stell said. "Larina has told me so much about you and the playhouse."

"I hope it was a good report," Lee said with his quick smile.

"Oh, yes. Please sit down. I've an idea or two to toss your way. I should say, Larina has. She thought of it."

Lee's quick eyes directed a quick look at Larina and she could see the interest on his face.

"Oh, Lee, I hope you'll think it's as great as I do," Larina said. "But it might be the answer to your problems and Aunt Stell's too."

140

Lee was bewildered. "What on earth could that be?" he wondered with a laugh.

"Does sound a little crazy," Larina admitted. "At least on the surface. So, I'll explain."

She was still explaining as Bertha put the coffee on the table. Their conversation carried all through the potful and she could see that Lee was sold on the idea from the very beginning.

"Do you think it would work?" Aunt Stella asked.

"We won't know until we try, will we? I can't see that either of us has anything to lose but everything to gain. We'll work out the details. The thing I want to know is, when do you want to do this?"

"The sooner the better," Aunt Stell said. "I've been thinking about it. If the first time is successful, maybe we could even promote a seasonal thing out of it. Sell season tickets—that is if that would be agreeable to you, Mr. Tyler."

Lee nodded. "Of course! We'd love to play to a full house every night we perform!"

"I'll have to clear this with the committee, of course, but I'm meeting with them this afternoon and I'm sure they'll like the idea. When do you put on your first play, Mr. Tyler?"

"It's set for next weekend. Would that give you enough time?"

"We'll move fast!" Aunt Stella promised. "We'll advertise every way we can think of."

"And I'll have Nollie put some additional information on our advertising and posters."

"I'll get approval of the committee and be in touch with you later this afternoon."

"Good," Lee said. "Good!"

Larina was beaming. It would all work out! For Jimmy. For all the children at the Home. It would mean some hard work for them all, but they'd do it. The meeting took on an air of gaiety and Larina could see that Aunt Stell liked Lee very much. He was direct and polite and there was always a vitality about him that was attractive.

Before he left, Larina invited him to see her studio.

"It's her pride and joy, Lee," Aunt Stell said.

Lee looked about the studio with interest, asked several intelligent questions and then asked to see the painting that was covered under her easel.

"It's not quite finished, but I suppose you can see it," Larina said.

When she uncovered it and revealed Sutton's portrait, Lee scowled.

"I know him. Sutton Ward. The playboy."

"My next-door neighbor," she said. "Attractive, don't you think?"

"I suppose, from a woman's eyes," Lee said angrily.

"He made an interesting study. I enjoyed working on it. I've still a little to finish, as you can see."

Lee's hazel eyes were sparking.

"Are you interested in him? Seriously?"

Larina re-covered the painting. "I'm—I'm not interested in anyone right now," she answered.

"I don't think I believe you."

"Then don't."

"Okay," Lee nodded.

They stared at each other tensely. Beyond the window, the surf rolled and the music of it drifted to them. Larina relaxed.

"Oh, Lee, why are we fighting?"

Lee was slower to forget about it. "I don't think I like Sutton Ward."

"You don't know him."

"And you do?"

Larina bit her lip. In a way she did. In some says, she felt as if she knew him very well, but then in others she didn't. Why did he carry a gun and why wouldn't he tell her? They had parted in anger yesterday. It worried her, much more than she wanted to admit to herself. She had caught herself looking over to his house several times. But it had been quiet there all morning and she had not seen him.

"There's something smooth and slippery about him," Lee said with a frown. "He paid me a visit, you know. But I got the distinct feeling he wasn't really interested in what we were doing there. But he was sure looking us over. And he was interested in meeting Nollie, of all people."

"Nollie's reputation is worldwide, you know," Larina said, making a face that made Lee smile at last.

"I've a hunch that Nollie does a little gambling on the side and I've heard the same about Sutton Ward. What else could it be? They're about as different as two people can be."

"Speaking of Nollie, will he have time to change all the posters? Perhaps I could help tomorrow, provided the committee decides to go along with the idea."

"I'd appreciate your help," Lee said. "You know how many posters we've put around town. They'll all have to be changed and the advertisements in the papers too."

"I'll be there," she promised. "Bright and early. So warn Nollie."

They walked out of the studio. The sun was brilliant and hot. But by now Larina had grown accustomed to it and she could look around without squinting or the need of sunglasses.

Lee went back inside to thank Aunt Stell for the coffee and say good-bye. Soon, Larina heard the sound of his old car pulling away.

"What a nice young man!" Aunt Stell said.

"Now, Aunt Stell—"

She held up her hand. "Oh, I wouldn't meddle. Not in a million years. But he's so different from Sutton!"

Larina knew she should go back to work in her studio, but today she wasn't in the mood. Perhaps it was talking so much about the Home that made her restless. She realized suddenly that she wanted to see Jimmy again. It was a perfect day and there was time! Why not arrange to have him come for a picnic lunch and an afternoon on the beach?

Reaching for the phone, she made arrangements, asked Bertha to fix the lunch and drove to the Home to pick up the dark-haired boy.

When she got there, he was jumping up and down in excitement.

"Larina! Larina!" he shouted. He came running to her, full of talk and laughter.

"All ready?" she asked.

"Oh, yes! Is the dog there?"

"I'm sure we can find him. And seashells. We'll watch the boats. We'll swim. Build sand castles. Eat all sorts of things Bertha will fix—oh, we'll have a great afternoon. I promise!"

It wasn't a promise hard to keep. Jimmy took one look at Sea Mist, at the blue waters of the Gulf and his eyes grew rounder and rounder.

Bertha had a basket lunch ready and with Jimmy helping her carry it, they walked down to the water.

It was one of those perfect days with white fleecy clouds floating, a clear horizon, the hot, white sand so smooth and clean, the gulls eyeing their basket with hungry interest and flapping their wings overhead. Jimmy put his hand in hers and his brown eyes flashed with excitement.

Since it was nearly noon, they ate the lunch first. Jimmy devoured more than his share, polishing off two pieces of Bertha's chocolate cake, leaving brown sticky smears on his face. Then there was the long walk, hand in hand, and the joy when the dog joined them. There were heaps and heaps of shells put in the plastic pail and proudly carried with them. There was the sailboat, skimming the water that caught Jimmy's attention and held him, rooted, until it slid on and nearly out of sight. It was sun, water, salt air, gulls, boats, shells, laughter, games of tag, sand castles built and washed out in the tide and it was above all, a warmth and friendliness that Larina knew she would treasure all the days of her life.

"Oh, Jimmy, Jimmy!" she murmured.

He gave her a salty, sandy hug and whispered in her ear. "You're pretty. Like my mommie."

It nearly tore her heart out. She hugged him fiercely.

"Oh, Jimmy, soon, someone will take you away from me."

"*You* adopt me!"

She laughed and took his face in her hands. "I wish I could. But you have to be married for that."

"Oh."

He puzzled over that for a moment and then forgot it

as he spied a starfish that had been washed up to the beach. For ten minutes, he poked, prodded, and examined it.

About three, she took him to see her studio. Someday she would make a series of sketches of him. If only she could catch that lively personality, those solemn eyes, that wonderful little grin! Then all too soon, it was time to take him home. He was tired and relaxed, happy. When they reached the Home, he had fallen sound asleep. Lifting him into her arms, she carried him inside.

Reluctantly, she turned him over to the woman in charge and bent down to kiss his forehead.

"Tell him good-bye for me when he wakes up, will you?"

"Yes, Miss Goodwin. He must have had a wonderful afternoon."

"I hope so."

Larina drove back to her studio. Thre was still time to do a little work and the hours spent with Jimmy had mellowed her. Her mood was ripe for the canvas.

She uncovered the unfinished painting of Sutton. Perhaps she shouldn't have been so angry with him. Perhaps his explanation had been truthful. But it made her nervous, knowing he often carried a gun. Somehow, she had expected him to join her early this morning on the beach when she went on her usual shell hunting walk. But he hadn't. Only the little dog, who lived somewhere up the beach, had joined her. He always trotted along happily beside her. She had grown used to him coming every morning, bouncing along, ears flapping, barking his greeting.

She couldn't finish the portrait of Sutton. Right at the moment, her feelings were too mixed about him. But she wanted to do an interior painting of the studio, just for fun, and so, she began that. It wouldn't be a large painting and it wouldn't take long to do.

She was well into it when there was a knock at her door.

"Who is it?"

"Messenger."

She frowned. What on earth. . . ? Going to open the

screen door, she took the white envelope a messenger boy extended to her.

"Sign here, please."

She signed her name and the boy tipped his cap. Then he was gone. She recognized the handwriting on the envelope. Bert! It was from Bert!

Ripping into it, she was disappointed to find only three brief lines. They read, "I'm fine. Don't worry about me. I'll be in touch."

Where was he? Surely somewhere in Gull Haven. But why the hiding? What was she going to do about it? If only she knew more about it! Why had he been so maddeningly vague?

She read and reread the note and studied the stationery, but there was no letterhead, no address, just plain, white paper. Why hadn't she thought to question the messenger? But then he was gone before she realized the letter was from Bert. Besides, he probably wouldn't have been able to tell her anything. For some reason, Bert was being very mysterious.

She went back to her work. As she painted, she began to remember the hours she'd spent in the room with Sutton, and soon her anger with him dissipated. She never could stay angry with anyone very long. They'd had some nice times here. Over lunch. The rainy day. The talk and laughter they'd shared. And yes—the love.

Her hand paused over her canvas and she asked herself, "Do I love him? Do I? But what about John? Yes, what about John?"

"Hello, in there!"

"Sutton!"

He stood in the doorway, hesitant. They looked at each other.

"Have you forgiven me?" he asked.

She laughed. "Yes."

"Good."

He was wearing casual clothes. Perhaps he'd been out fishing. She was relieved that he had no inner coat-pocket in which to conceal a gun. Without a word, he came to take her in his arms, paint-smeared smock and all. His kiss was long and warm.

"How are you?" he asked.

"All right."

"I'm sorry about yesterday."

"So am I."

"Can we forget it? Put it behind us?"

"I don't really know. Can we?"

"Let's try," he urged.

"All right."

He kissed her again and the last bit of her anger was gone.

"What's this you're doing?"

"Just a little painting of the studio."

He looked at it with a studious expression on his handsome face. "No, Larina, it's more than a studio. It's our room. Yours and mine."

His gray eyes were warm when he looked at her. "I love the painting. It makes me remember the times I've been here."

"You really haven't been here that often," she pointed out, trying hard to be practical.

"Does it matter? It's what has happened in those few times that really counts." He seemed unusually gay and at ease today, less tense.

"Oh, Sutton, what am I to do with you?"

"I told you once. Just love me."

The moment was very quiet as they looked at each other. Then Larina made herself move out of his arms. Sutton sighed.

"We seem to be able to go just so far, don't we, Larina? Then you start putting up that brick wall between us."

"Sorry," she murmured.

"Have you heard from John?"

"No."

"Do you think you will?"

"Perhaps not," she admitted.

"Doesn't that tell you anything?"

"No. John's—well, he gets wrapped up in things, time gets away from him. He becomes so engrossed in that one thing—"

"No man should be so engrossed that he forgets the woman he loves."

"I'll have a letter soon. I'm sure of it."

"Yes. Perhaps you will," Sutton sighed. "Speaking of letters, I thought I saw a messenger just leaving as I drove up. I hope you didn't have bad news or anything."

Larina started. She should have destroyed the letter. Where had she put it? It wouldn't do for Aunt Stell to find it by accident, or anyone else for that matter! Sutton was waiting for an answer.

"Oh, no. Nothing bad. Just—just some banking business, something for Uncle Ernie."

"Oh, is he coming home?"

Larina licked her lips. That hadn't been a very successful little white lie.

"I don't know. I believe Aunt Stell is going to take care of it."

"Oh, I see. Well, good. Messengers and Western Union delivery boys always give me a fright. Old-fashioned of me, isn't it?"

"Yes," she laughed. "And I never thought of you as being old-fashioned!"

The subject was safely past. Putting away her work materials, she tidied the studio and when Sutton wasn't looking, she found Bert's letter and tucked it away out of sight. She would dispose of it later.

"Let's take a walk," Sutton suggested.

"All right."

She liked walking the beach anytime and somehow, with Sutton, it was even more exciting. Now and then, his hand brushed hers and always, his gaze was warm and direct when he looked at her. He seemed to walk a little stronger and there was a confidence about him that she liked. Now and then, he looked to the sea, as if searching for a particular sight or boat.

When they turned back at last and he saw her home, he asked to see her that night for dinner.

He had never made a date for the nighttime before and she was surprised.

"Tonight!"

"Surprised? Yes, tonight. We've never been out at night, have we? Usually, I must rest or I'm tied up with business affairs. Tonight—thanks to a certain man—I'm free."

"I don't understand."

"You're not supposed to," he laughed. "Will you come?"

"All right."

"Good! Seven-thirty?"

"I'll be ready."

"This will be a night to remember, Larina. I promise you that."

XVIII

AUNT STELLA'S COMMITTEE decided to join forces with Lee's playhouse, effective immediately. Larina took time to go and see Lee and tell him the good news.

The place was quiet when she reached it. Stepping inside, she looked around. Even Nollie was absent. But she heard voices coming from Lee's office.

Going there quickly, for she had little time, she was about to knock on the door when it opened and Angel Jones stepped out.

"Oh, Larina!" Angel said with a start. "You startled me!"

"Sorry. Is Lee here? I just want to see him for a minute."

Lee was dabbing at his face with a handkerchief. Angel disappeared quickly. Lee looked as startled as Angel had.

"Why, Larina! What brings you?"

"News," Larina said. "Aunt Stell's committee loves the idea."

Lee sat down behind his desk with a grin. "Good! Good! That's great, Larina. I'll have Nollie get right on the changes on the posters."

"I'll help if I can. Maybe tomorrow morning," Larina said.

"Good! I'll tell him to plan on you."

Lee seemed nervous. Or was he just excited with her news? She didn't know. Was that a little smudge of lipstick at the corner of his mouth?

Her eyebrows went up. Lee and Angel? What else could she think.

"I have to be going," she said quickly.

"But why? Stay. Have supper with me."

"I can't."

"Why the rush?" he asked.

"Date," she replied.

"Oh! With Sutton Ward?" he asked angrily.

"Yes. Matter of fact."

Lee's hazel eyes were sparking with fire when she waved good-bye and walked swiftly out of the playhouse. But she noticed that Angel was still there, pretending to be busy up on the stage. If Angel had her way, Lee would soon forget his anger.

Driving home, Larina saw that she had only a few minutes to get ready for her date with Sutton. She selected a pretty pink dress and matching accessories. Now and then, she paused to look out at the ocean, loving the sight of the water in the late afternoon. She watched the gulls, white-winged and graceful, swooping down to settle on the beach or to go chasing after the fishing boats as they came home with their day's catch.

While Aunt Stell ate dinner, Larina briefly joined her. "I wish your uncle could be here for the opening," Aunt Stell said wistfully. "Not that he ever cared much for such things, but it would be nice to have him home again."

"Why, Aunt Stell!" Larina teased. "I thought you liked having him out of the house, so you can have the cleaners in and the painters—"

Aunt Stell looked sheepish. "I'm afraid you've found me out. That was just a lot of talk to bolster my own spirits."

"Let's phone him!" Larina said. "Let's ask him to come home. He said he might jet back for a weekend. Why not?"

"Oh, that's such an extravagance—"

Larina laughed. "I'm sure Uncle Ernie can afford it. I'd love talking to him, wouldn't you?"

"Well—yes—"

"I'll try, right this very minute!"

Larina put in the call and it took several minutes but soon, she had Uncle Ernie on the line.

"Hello, Uncle Ernie!"

"Larina? Is that you? Is something wrong? Is Stell all right?"

"Nothing's wrong. We just thought we'd talk to you. How are you?"

"Fine. Busy. Very busy. Working hard so I can get back and play with you on the beach," Uncle Ernie laughed. "Are you behaving yourself?"

"Of course! How are you, Uncle Ernie?"

"Just homesick, that's all."

"That's good!"

"Good!" he snorted. "What sort of nonsense is that?"

"If you're homesick, you're more apt to fall in with our plans," Larina laughed. "I'll let Aunt Stell tell you about them. I'm going out and my date's ringing the bell right this minute. I miss you, Uncle Ernie. Hurry home."

"Date? Who's taking you out?" he asked. "Larina—"

She laughed and handed the receiver to her aunt. "You can persuade him, Aunt Stell. I'm sure of it."

Then Larina waved good-bye and went to answer the door. Sutton Ward stood there in a light summer suit, his black hair brushed and glossy. His gray eyes devoured her.

"Hmm! Beautiful," he said. "Shall we go?"

He offered his arm. It was fun to step out into the dusk of a Florida summer evening on the arm of such an attractive man. She wouldn't wonder if the pistol was in his inside coat pocket. She wouldn't think about that at all.

"I hope you'll like the evening I have planned," he said.

"I'm sure I will," she replied.

"I promised something special. At least, it will be different."

He handed her into his sports car and then they were on their way. She wondered if Aunt Stell was still talking to Uncle Ernie and what he was going to say when he found out she was going out with Sutton Ward. Well, she didn't care! She liked Sutton. Whether anyone else did or not!

They drove leisurely down Beach Front Road. Sutton

was humming softly to himself. Now and then, he flashed her a smile.

"You seem very happy tonight, Sutton."

"I am," he said. "Things seem right with the world for me tonight."

"I like you like this."

"I'm glad."

"Why can't you always be so lighthearted and cheerful?"

A frown passed over his face and he shook his head.

"Life just wasn't made that way, Larina. Was it?"

"I suppose not. At least, not for some."

"I hope you like the sea," he said, changing the subject.

"Yes. You know I do."

"I mean, not just as seen from the beach. I mean to be out on it!"

"Of course, I do! Are we going for a cruise?"

Sutton gave her a quick grin. His gray eyes were bright and warm.

"Yes."

They were driving toward the public docks. Leaving the car in the parking lot, they walked to a waiting yacht.

"We're ready, Harry. Shove off at your pleasure."

Sutton helped her aboard the boat. Then with a steadying hand, they went below. There, the table was laid and she knew that food was waiting to be served.

"I had one of the hotel chefs prepare this. I'm hoping that you'll like what I ordered."

They heard the motor start and the skipper, Harry, eased the boat gently out from the dock.

"I told Harry to take us out a few miles and then stop. We'll eat in the middle of the Gulf, with no one staring at us or eavesdropping or wondering who that lovely girl is that I have with me!" Sutton said.

He turned on a tape player and quiet music flowed. Sitting down beside her on the comfortable divan, he reached for her hand.

"In a little while, we'll go up on top and watch the last

of the sunset," he said. "But I wanted these moments with you first."

He put his arm around her. Then, with a long-fingered hand, he turned her to face him. His gray eyes burned and she saw that he was serious. Deadly serious.

"I love you, Larina. I never expected this to happen. It was not part of my plan. But it's happened, and now I have to do something about it."

"Do you?" she asked.

"Yes."

His kiss was fiery and exciting. When he let her go at last, he gave her a gentle smile.

"You do care for me, Larina, don't you?"

She got to her feet. How did she answer that when she didn't really know herself?

"There are so many things about you, Sutton. Things I don't understand."

"Trust me," he said. "And tonight, let's not discuss them. Let's just have the night to remember. All right?"

She found herself nodding.

"All right, Sutton. Just the night to remember."

"Good," he nodded. "Now, let's go up on deck and watch the sunset. Then soon, we'll eat dinner and then— well, I have many things to say to you."

The sunset was vibrant. Sunsets in Florida were often colorful and it was like watching a play develop, scene by scene, act by act, as the sun dropped further and further into the horizon, leaving behind a sky stained with unbelievable changing colors.

Harry piloted the boat out from the shore and soon Gull Haven had all but been lost. Water was all around them. They seemed to be isolated from the rest of the world.

When the last of the sun had slipped away from them, Sutton took her arm.

"Shall we dine, darling?" he asked.

The food had been put in a warming oven and Sutton proved awkward in serving it, so Larina took over the task. There was a chilled salad in the icebox and a full course dinner in the oven. They ate the salad, saying little. The magic of the sea and the night was weaving its way in and around Larina's heart. What woman wouldn't respond to something like this?

Sutton toasted her.

"To the loveliest girl I know."

"Thank you, Sutton."

"And also, to the girl I love," he replied.

The food was delicious. They ate hungrily and Sutton was delighted that she was pleased.

"Oh, Sutton, I've never had a date like this before!"

"I tried to be original."

"I've never even been on a yacht. I've been on Uncle Ernie's cabin cruiser, but it isn't anything like this. Is the boat yours?"

"No. I've only leased it for tonight. If you want it, I'll buy it for you."

"Would you really?"

He squeezed her hand. "Yes, darling, I would. I'd give you the world if I could. I'd give you anything you wanted. Most of all, I'd like to give you my heart, here and now."

She met his gray eyes. He was serious. She couldn't doubt him, even when she knew she probably should.

"In a few days, Larina, I'll tell you everything there is to tell about myself. But until then, I have to ask you to trust me, to have faith in me. I love you, Larina. And I never thought it would happen, but I find myself wanting to be married."

She gasped. At that, he laughed.

"Why did you think I brought you here like this? Didn't I tell you it would be a night to remember?"

"Yes, but—"

"Will you marry me, Larina?"

Everything had come too fast for her. How long ago had it been when she'd first met Sutton Ward on the beach? Not long. Yet in many ways, it had been years.

"Sutton, I don't know what to say."

"Then say nothing. Think about it. Until, say—midnight," he told her with a smile. "At the witching hour, I'll ask again."

The music played softly. The boat rocked ever so gently and the sea air came in the open portholes. The candles burned low. The last of the food was gone. Sutton's hand held hers across the table.

There was a discreet knock and Harry's voice called to Sutton.

"Mr. Ward, may I see you for a minute? It's important. I've just had a radio message."

Sutton frowned. It seemed his hand grew cold in hers as he sat there for a moment, reluctant to leave her.

"Mr. Ward!"

"Yes, I'm coming. In a minute, Harry."

He looked at Larina. With a shake of his head, he sighed.

"I don't know what's come up. Sorry."

"I'll go up with you, if you don't mind. I'd like to see the sea at night."

He led her up the stairs and she took a deck chair, leaned back and looked at the stars overhead. They seemed so close, so rich, so compelling.

To the far end of the boat, she saw Sutton and Harry huddling together.

"Escaped!" she heard Sutton say angrily. "It can't be!"

"That's the message, sir."

"Head back to Gull Haven," Sutton said urgently. "As fast as this boat will go!"

"Yes, sir!"

"Sutton, what is it?" Larina called. "What's happened?"

Sutton was angry. His fists were knotted and in the light coming from the cabin below, she saw the hard set of his jaw.

"Ever have a prize bird in a cage?" he asked. "Ever have it get away?"

"No."

"Well, it's happened to me. Of all the rotten luck—"

"I don't understand, Sutton."

He seemed to have forgotten her. He moved to the railing and stood there, gripping it, muttering to himself, eyes fastened on the approaching lights of Gull Haven. Harry was wasting no time.

Sutton was a different person altogether and it frightened her. She shivered, even though the night was warm. How could the lovely, lovely evening have come to this?

XIX

As THE LIGHTS of Gull Haven grew nearer and nearer it seemed to Larina that Sutton grew more quiet. When Harry had finally tied up at the dock, Sutton reached a hand to her.

"Come along, Larina. I'll see you home."

"Are you sure you have the time?" she asked.

His gray eyes flickered. "I'll see you home," he said evenly.

But the gaiety of just an hour ago, the closeness they had shared, seemed to be forgotten. He walked swiftly to his car. Larina had never known him to drive so fast through the streets.

Then at last, she saw they were nearing Beach Front Road and she was relieved. When Sutton was like this, so preoccupied and tense, it was like being with a stranger. They pulled into the driveway at Sea Mist and Sutton turned to her.

"Larina, I'm sorry. I wish it hadn't happened," Sutton said. He bent his head and kissed her fleetingly. "I'll see you to the door."

"Never mind," she said. "You're in a hurry—"

"Thank you for being so understanding, Larina."

But she wasn't understanding any of it! She watched as he drove away until the red taillights on his car disappeared. Standing there, she tried to put aside the hurt she felt, but she couldn't. Everything had been so splendid until the radio message had come in. What on earth could have happened? Why was Sutton so mysterious about it all?

With a shudder, she remembered the gun she'd found

in his pocket. She remembered how everyone thought he was a gambler. What sort of people was he mixed up with anyway?

Going inside, she found Aunt Stell still up.

"Hello, Aunt Stell."

"My, you're home early!"

"Yes."

"Something wrong?"

It was on the tip of her tongue to tell her aunt everything but she changed her mind.

She shook her head. "No. You seem excited about something."

Aunt Stell laughed. "He's coming, Larina. He's coming!"

"Uncle Ernie?"

"Yes!"

"I knew you could persuade him!"

"His flight will be in at eleven o'clock next Saturday morning. He'll attend the opening with us."

"That's the best news I've heard in ages," she said. "I miss him when he's not here."

Perhaps when he came she could tell him about Sutton's mysterious behavior. Perhaps, she would even tell him that Bert was in town and in trouble. No. She couldn't do that. She couldn't betray Bert's trust in her.

When she went to bed that night, Larina saw that Sutton's house was still dark. Was he still out looking for the prize bird that had flown the cage? She sighed. None of it made a bit of sense to her!

For the next few days, she did not see Sutton and she busied herself at the playhouse. There was much to do to get the grand opening under way and to promote the productions as an aid to charity. Lee seemed to be everywhere at once, shouting orders with enthusiasm, supervising this, and ordering that. Everyone stepped to it and even Larina could see that things were beginning to shape up.

She tried to join the enthusiasm with her usual vigor, but found it hard to do. Sutton weighed heavily on her heart and her mind. She had not seen him since the night of their cruise nor had she heard from him. What could he be doing?

Late one afternoon, after working at the playhouse, Larina decided to take a breather and walked out to the beach. Everything inside was hectic. They were getting down to the wire. Tonight was the dress rehearsal and tomorrow night they would have their grand opening. She lingered there several minutes and was surprised when she saw Lee coming from the direction of the Bleaker house. What could he be doing over there? When he saw her, he came up short, then with a smile, he walked toward her.

"Hi."

"What were you doing over there?" Larina wondered.

Lee shrugged. "Nothing, really. Just getting some fresh air. By the way, you haven't seen Nollie, have you?"

"No."

"When I need him the most, he does the disappearing act!" Lee said angrily.

"You're excited about the opening, aren't you?" Larina asked.

Lee nodded and his hazel eyes were watching her closely.

"Yes. Very. It's been a dream of mine to do this sort of thing. Now—it's happening. Even if we flop, it's been an experience I won't soon forget."

He caught her hand in his. "Let's walk down to the water. I'd like to talk to you, Larina. Seriously."

She was wary when his voice took on this tone. But he tugged her along until they were well out of the sight of the playhouse.

"Larina—I know I made a mess of things, starting out the way I did with you. I don't want that. I want something deeper, truer. I'm trying to tell you that I love you, Larina."

"Oh, Lee—"

He kissed her. Deeply, emotionally. It wouldn't be hard to succumb to a man like Lee. But she couldn't. She didn't want to be involved. Not after that night of the cruise with Sutton. He had hurt her badly. One minute he had been asking her to marry him; the next, he was like a stranger. How could he have done that to her?

"Larina—"

She shook her head and met Lee's hazel eyes.

"I'm sorry, Lee. It just won't work."

He gripped her by the shoulders. "It has to work! Larina, I care for you."

It would be easy to believe him. At the moment, perhaps he even believed himself.

"What about Angel?"

Lee flushed at that. "Larina, listen, please—"

"No. I only want to be your friend, Lee. Nothing more."

He stared at her and she saw the flush on his face deepen.

"Let's go back, Lee. You've got work to do and I have to get home."

She began walking away, and after a moment, Lee came with her, saying nothing, shoulders set rigidly. They passed the old Bleaker house and Larina darted a look at it. What had Lee really been doing over there?

As they approached the playhouse, they saw Nollie motioning to them.

"Hey, man!" Nollie shouted, waving a piece of paper. "I've got news. We're a sellout."

Lee blinked. "You're kidding. Nollie, if this is your idea of a joke—"

"No joke!" Nollie said. "Those ladies on that committee really went to town and sold tickets. We've even got an advance sale on the next two performances!"

Lee laughed. "Well, what do you know!"

"That's wonderful news, Lee," Larina said happily. "For everyone."

"It sure is! Hey, I've got to tell the rest of them."

Lee hurried away inside the theatre, shouting as he went. Angel came running to meet him and linked her arm through his. Lee didn't seem to mind at all.

"Well, Nollie, the big night will soon be upon us," Larina said.

Nollie rubbed his crew cut red hair. "Yeah, I know."

"You don't sound happy," Larina teased. "I thought you were dying to get on the stage."

"Oh, sure, I am," Nollie said.

But he sounded vague, preoccupied. It wasn't like Nollie at all.

Larina lingered at the playhouse a little while longer and decided that they really didn't need her services anymore. Things were ready to roll for tomorrow night.

It was dark when she went outside and got in the convertible. The night was brilliant with stars but there was no moon. The Gulf seemed inky black as she caught glimpses of it through the palms. She drove slowly along Beach Front Road, past the gloomy old Bleaker house and toward Sea Mist.

"Larina, don't turn around. Keep your eyes straight ahead!" a voice said behind her.

She was so startled that for a moment the car swerved on the street.

"Hey, take it easy. It's me, Bert. I'm on the floor. Out of sight."

"Bert!"

"Now just drive like you always do. Go in the garage and close the door. I must not be seen. Do you understand that?"

"Bert, I don't know what you're doing or what you're talking about, but if you don't give me some answers soon—"

"Larina, it might mean my life! Does that make it any clearer?" he asked hoarsely.

"Oh, Bert—"

"Now don't get weepy on me. You have to help me. You're the only one I can trust. Will you do as I say?"

"Of course!" she said.

"Good. Once I get in the garage, I'll wait until everyone's gone to bed and then I'll slip into the house and go up to my room. If you can manage to get some food up there to me, I'd sure appreciate it."

"All right."

"Whatever you do, don't let your next-door neighbor see me."

"Sutton?" she asked with surprise. "What's Sutton got to do with this?"

She was tense now, hands clenching the steering wheel so hard that her fingers were aching.

At last, she saw the familiar roof of Sea Mist and began to breathe faster. Just a few more feet and she would safely be past Sutton's place. His house was still dark. She didn't think he'd been home since the night of their cruise. She drove into the garage, cut the motor and turned off the lights.

"Don't look back here," Bert said. "Just act natural. They may be watching you."

She took her purse and walked swiftly past the car and to the door. Then stepping out into the black night, she pulled the door down. Her heart was thundering. What did Bert mean, someone might be watching? Perhaps someone from Sutton's darkened house? The thought only made her all the more nervous.

She let herself in with the key Aunt Stell had given her. Bertha was still in the kitchen, doing the dinner dishes. Aunt Stell was on the phone.

Glancing at her watch, Larina saw that it was going to be a long evening before everyone retired. Poor Bert, hiding in that hot garage!

Aunt Stell hung up.

"Oh, Larina, a letter came for you. Special delivery. From your father."

"Dad?" she asked with alarm. "Is something wrong?"

"I suggest you open it and find out," Aunt Stell said.

She pressed the letter into Larina's hand. She tore into it anxiously. Then she found another smaller envelope inside. It was addressed to her in John's handwriting.

"John!" she murmured. "It's from John. I think I'll take it up to my room to read, Aunt Stell."

"Yes. You do that."

Clutching it tightly in her hand, she hurried up the carpeted stairs. For a moment, she hesitated about opening it. Then with nervous fingers, she tore it open and drew out the single sheet of paper inside.

It took only a moment to read. The message was very terse and to the point.

"Just to let you know that I'm marrying an old child-hood sweetheart in August. Don't know how else to say it, except directly. We had some great times and I wish you all the luck and happiness in the world."

It was signed, "Your friend, John."

XX

IT WAS NEARLY MIDNIGHT. Larina had spent all evening by her window, staring out at the sea, John's letter in her hand. So, it was over. Dad had been right. She had been wrong about him.

But how did she really feel about it? Then, with a tired smile, she realized that she no longer cared. For the fact of it was, she had fallen in love with Sutton Ward, and she had fallen hard.

Then a cloud of doom settled over her. How could she love a man she knew so little about, whom Bert was insinuating might be spying on them?

She looked at her watch. Twelve thirty. The house had been quiet for nearly an hour. Had she heard a furtive step on the stairs? Going to her door, she peered out. A hand came out of the darkness and covered her mouth.

"Sh!" Bert hissed in her ear. "Not a sound. Come to my room and we'll talk."

They went quietly into his room and closed the door. Bert would not risk a light.

"We can talk here," he said in a low voice. "No one will hear us. The surf is too noisy."

"Bert! Where have you been? Why didn't you come sooner? I've been worried sick about you."

Bert hunched his shoulders. "I've got to know one thing, Larina. Did you tell anyone I was home? Anyone?"

"No. Of course not."

"You didn't tell Mother or Nick or Bertha—"

"No!"

"And you didn't tell Sutton Ward?"

"Of course not! Bert, what's this got to do with Sutton?"

Bert laughed harshly. "Everything. Just everything."

"Please, won't you explain?"

"Sure," Bert said. "I guess it's time. I'll tell you what I can. It's not especially pretty, Larina. But first, I'm starving. Would you go down and raid the kitchen?"

"Yes. Just a minute."

She hurried down the steps. Often, she had come down for a glass of milk or a sandwich and if anyone heard her now, they wouldn't think it odd.

She grabbed a couple of pieces of fruit from the bowl on the table, made two thick sandwiches, took a carton of milk and hurried back upstairs. Bert was waiting for her and he ate hungrily while she paced the floor, waiting for an explanation.

"Man, was that good!" Bert sighed. "Thanks, Larina. I've had nothing but stolen oranges from Peterson's trees."

"You've been at the grove? But I went there looking for you and you weren't there—"

"I've been there the past few days," he said. "And before that, I was being held a prisoner in a motel on the edge of town by Sutton and his men."

"Sutton and his men!"

"Sh! Keep your voice down," Bert warned. "Yes, Sutton and his men. They wanted some information about Juan Gonzales."

Larina shook her head in bewilderment. "But who is that?"

Bert laughed softly. "I pretended I didn't know. But of course, I did. You got my message, didn't you?"

"Yes."

"I told them that if they'd just let me get in touch with you, I'd tell them what I knew. Well, I told them some things, but it was just a made-up story. They found it out, of course. They're sharp boys, I'll give them that."

"Bert—"

He came to put a hand on her shoulder. "Easy, I'm getting to it. You know I went to Mexico. You know once in awhile I do something stupid, like taking part in a card game or something like that. This started out harmless enough. There were four other guys. One of them was Juan Gonzales. The rest were his buddies."

"I wish you wouldn't gamble, Bert. You know you shouldn't."

"I won't ever again. That's a promise. I've learned my lesson. But to get on with my story, one of the men let some information slip and since I've been around a little, I caught on. I did a little investigating later and learned they were planning on smuggling a large drug shipment into Florida in a couple of weeks. My luck didn't hold out. They caught me eavesdropping and I barely escaped with my hide! I don't know yet how I managed to get away from them!"

"Oh, Bert!"

"Anyway, I did. I had to leave Mexico with hardly a cent in my pocket. I managed to get home and I came to you for help. I was sure some of Juan's gang were here and would probably have been warned about me. So, I had to be careful. I want to get Juan Gonzales if it's the last thing I do! I'd like to nip this whole sordid mess in the bud! Well, I nosed around a little, following the leads I had and that's when I ran into Sutton Ward and his men."

"Sutton?"

"They picked me up on the beach and took me to the Flamingo Motel. I've been there, undergoing all kinds of questioning."

"But why?" Larina asked, astonished. "I don't understand. Maybe I'm a little dumb—"

"Sutton knew I was after Juan. They couldn't afford to have anything go wrong. There was too much at stake. Sutton and his men are Juan's contacts in Florida! Don't you see?"

Larina was so stunned that for a moment she couldn't say anything. Head spinning and her heart knocking, she moved to the window and leaned against it.

"You mean, Sutton is—in on the drug smuggling?"

"Has to be. Why else would he have picked me up?

They were afraid I'd go to the police with what I knew. They couldn't let that happen."

"And now, Sutton is looking for you?"

Bert sighed. "Yes. He's looking for me all right! A time or two I thought my number was up, but I was able to give them the slip. Then I decided the smart thing to do was to come home, hide right under his nose. He wouldn't expect that."

She couldn't comprehend it all. Sutton dealing in drugs! She shuddered. Suddenly, she was seeing Jimmy's big brown eyes and the sadness that came to his face when he spoke of his mother, a woman who had died because of drugs.

Sutton, oh, Sutton!

Hot tears slid down her cheeks. She covered her face with her hands for a moment, wishing she could wake up from the nightmare. Bert came to stand beside her.

"You'll keep quiet about my being here, won't you? I don't want Mother or Bertha or Nick to know I'm here. It's safer that way."

She nodded slowly.

"Of course, I'll keep quiet. But Bert, this is dangerous! Why don't you phone the police?"

"I considered it," Bert said. "But I don't want to risk it. If the police started hanging round, it would tip them off sure. Sutton and his men would get wise and they'd call off the whole deal."

"Oh, I wish they would!"

"No!" Bert said sharply. "I want them to make the delivery. I want to be there and catch them. I want Juan and Sutton and all those men to go to prison for their dirty work!"

"But what can you do alone, Bert?"

"Don't worry, I've got it all worked out. Now, relax. Trust me. And whatever you do, keep your mouth shut!"

"Like a clam," she said tiredly.

Bert sank to the bed with a sigh. "I'm beat, Larina. Dead for sleep. Don't worry, I know what I'm doing."

"But where's the contact point?" she asked. "Bert—"

"It's the most unlikely part of the whole thing. But it's

something Juan would do. He thinks he's so darned smart! Pulling it off right under everybody's nose—"

In the next instant, he was asleep. Larina lifted his feet up and stood for a moment looking down at him. Then she tiptoed out of the room.

She could not sleep. The night was spent before the windows staring at the Gulf. So peaceful. So lovely. Yet now, it was almost ugly—because of Sutton and what he really was. Not just a playboy and gambler, but a man who dealt in drugs.

She was so sick at heart that she couldn't believe that only a few hours ago she was telling herself that she loved him, no matter what.

How could she love him now?

Slowly, her anguish gave way to anger. Never again would she be taken in by a smooth-talking, handsome man, no matter how he acted or what he said, or how he made her feel!

She ate little breakfast. Aunt Stell eyed her with concern.

"You're not ill?" she asked anxiously. "Not today of all days. Ernie will be home in a few hours and tonight's the big night at the playhouse."

"No. I'm all right, Aunt Stell."

"Oh, then it was the letter from John."

Larina had nearly forgotten about the letter from John Adair. But now, it could serve as a perfect excuse for her behavior.

"He's marrying someone else," she said.

Then she left the table abruptly and went out to the patio. But from there she could see Sutton's house and it only reminded her of what Bert had told her. Then going to her studio, she looked around the room she had loved. She and Sutton had shared so much here. Her eyes rested on the painting of the studio and somehow, it was a greater wrench to her heart than the portrait she'd done of Sutton.

On impulse, she snatched up the canvas, went to the house for her purse and car keys and drove away from Sea Mist. It took half an hour to reach Tish's shop with the painting in her hand.

Tish had just opened for business and was surprised to see her.

"Well, hi, Larina," she said. "How are you? I've been so busy at the playhouse, I've had time for nothing else."

"Hello, Tish," she said dully.

"Well, you're sure a bowl of sunshine this morning," Tish laughed. "Something wrong?"

"Would you sell this painting for me, Tish? Get as much as you can for it. I want to donate the proceeds to the Home."

"Of course I will. Say, this is very good, Larina! Are you sure you want to sell this one? You must have others—"

"I want to sell it!" she said firmly. "I never want to lay my eyes on that painting again!"

"All right," Tish shrugged. "Hey, where are you going? What's the hurry? Can't you take time for a cup of coffee—"

But Larina had fled. She couldn't stay there and make small talk. She wasn't capable of it today. But she was relieved that the painting was gone and she never had to look at it again. What she'd do with the portrait of Sutton, she didn't know. Perhaps take a knife and hack it to pieces!

She took time to drive by the Home. Perhaps seeing Jimmy would lift her spirits.

When he saw her convertible, he came striding toward her. He was sad today. She knew from the slope of his shoulders.

"Hello, Jimmy."

"Hello," he said quietly.

She got out of the car and knelt down beside him.

"What's wrong, Jimmy?"

"Some people came. They looked at me. But they didn't like me."

She could only guess that someone had thought about adopting him and had decided against it.

"I'm sorry, Jimmy."

Then there were tears rolling down his cheeks and she felt so helpless, so filled with anguish that she nearly cried herself.

"Oh, I wish Mommie hadn't died," he sobbed. "I wish she hadn't."

Larina knotted her fists. "So do I, honey. So do I."

She stayed there nearly an hour, trying to cheer him but she didn't succeed very well. Perhaps because her own heart was so heavy.

Then she had to leave him. It would soon be time for them to meet Uncle Ernie's plane.

"I'll come back again, soon," she promised.

"Tomorrow. Will you come tomorrow?"

"Yes, Jimmy, I'll come tomorrow."

Returning home, she went upstairs to her room. She paused outside Bert's door and pushed it open. But Bert wasn't there. Nor had he been there earlier. Where was he hiding? Perhaps down in the garage. Where else could he be?

There wasn't time to look for him. Nick was getting out the car. Aunt Stell was ready to go to the airport.

Uncle Ernie's flight was on time. In a few minutes, he was beside them, giving them a hug and a kiss and pressing small gifts into their hands.

"Something from London. Just for my two best girls. How's the wrist, Stell?" he asked.

"Fine. I'll get rid of the cast before you know it. You're looking fit as a fiddle."

"Things are going well. With a little luck, I can wind it up quicker than I had hoped," he said, beaming. "Ah, it's good to be home. I can smell that sea air already. But, Larina, you look a little pale. What's wrong?"

Aunt Stell motioned for him to keep quiet and when they had an opportunity, she saw her aunt whispering to him, no doubt telling him about the letter from John. It was simpler just to let him think that was what had upset her. How could she tell him that his son was home, hiding out from a gang of drug smugglers, that she had made the horrible mistake of falling in love with one of them?

Uncle Ernie was full of amusing stories. Aunt Stell laughed all the way home and Larina managed a smile or two.

"Now, what's all this about the playhouse?" Uncle Ernie asked.

"We've got a sell-out, Ernie," Aunt Stell told him. "Thanks to Larina, she just solved everyone's problems."

Everyone's but her own. With a sigh, Larina watched Nick maneuver the car through the heavy traffic. When she saw the roof of Sea Mist, she wondered if she could hold in the tears. But somehow, someway, she had to get through this day. She had to go to the opening at the playhouse, do all the right things, say all the right things.

Bertha had a light lunch ready for them. It seemed to last an eternity. Then, using an excuse that she wanted to do some work in her studio, she escaped.

The room was hot and she cranked open the windows, letting the sea air come in. For half a moment, she forgot all the terrible things that had happened and listened for the sound of Sutton's steps.

But he wouldn't be coming now. How could he have held Bert prisoner and made love to her at the same time? What kind of a man could do that? What kind of terrible, terrible man?

She didn't paint that day. There was no desire left in her. The summer was only off to a good beginning and already—for her—it had come to a crashing end. Perhaps she would go home to Riverdale. There, she wouldn't be reminded of Sutton. She knew Dad missed her. He would welcome her back. Yes, perhaps that was the solution. Just as soon as Aunt Stell shed her cast. Uncle Ernie was expecting to be home before long, too. She wouldn't be needed here much longer.

Somehow, she got through the afternoon. She even went for a walk with Uncle Ernie. He dropped an arm around her shoulder companionably.

"Too bad about John," he said quietly.

"Yes," she murmured.

He paused and looked out to the sea.

"Any more news on the drug smugglers?"

Her heart nearly stopped. She shook her head. "No."

"Nasty business," he concluded.

She bent and retrieved a shell, pretending to examine

it. Was Bert watching them furtively from his window? Was Sutton watching them too? A chill went over her.

"Let's go back, Uncle Ernie," she said. "I've got a few things to do before we go to the playhouse and Bertha's having an early dinner."

"Matter of fact, I could use a nap. This change in time gets me all fouled up!"

The play was to begin at eight. As Larina was dressing, she heard the *Mary Belle* starting up. Nick was taking her out! But why? Or was it Bert? She had not seen Bert all day nor did she know where he was. Had he left the house again? Was that him out there in the *Mary Belle*? Where was he going? Could tonight be the night?

Uncle Ernie was fussing at Aunt Stell to hurry, fearing they would be late. Larina was relieved that Uncle Ernie hadn't noticed the *Mary Belle* leaving the dock for if he questioned her, she was sorely afraid she'd tell all she knew. It was a heavy secret to carry.

"I'm ready at last," Aunt Stell announced.

"I'll drive you in the convertible," Larina said.

"Yes. Sounds like fun," Ernie agreed.

"Drive slowly, so you won't muss my hair," Aunt Stell told her.

Larina was as nervous as a treed cat. She licked her lips and tried not to look at Sutton's house as she went by. She kept telling herself how much she hated him for being what he was.

There was a good crowd gathering at the playhouse and Aunt Stell was beaming. Lee was handsome in a summer suit, his thick brown hair carefully brushed. If he seemed a bit cool toward Larina, she was too emotionally wrought to notice. The crowd gathered with a scraping of feet and shuffle of chairs. Then at last, the lights were dim and the curtain went up.

"That's the backdrop I painted, Uncle Ernie," Larina whispered.

"Beautiful!" he answered with a smile.

The play was going very well. Even Angel Jones did her role with a professional touch. Nollie was the clown that made everyone laugh. He was easily stealing the show.

When the curtain came down on the first act, the applause was loud and long. Five minutes passed, then ten. Larina checked her watch. Fifteen minutes! Something had gone wrong. The crowd was getting restless.

"Excuse me, Uncle Ernie," Larina said.

She slipped away backstage. There Lee was all but tearing out his hair and his eyes were flashing angrily.

"Where can he be? Has everyone looked, really looked?" he asked.

"Lee, what is it?" Larina asked.

"Nollie!" he roared angrily. "Who else? Nollie's done the disappearing act again!"

XXI

BERT HAD LEFT HIS ROOM early that day, fearful Bertha would discover him there. Unless his calculations were wrong, tonight was the night. His nerves tingled with anticipation. But he wasn't entirely stupid either. What could one man do against several?

With this thought in mind, he slipped downstairs, eased into the garage and took the inside stairs up to Nick's living quarters.

Tapping at the door, he pushed it open and stepped in. Nick was having a late cup of coffee. He blinked with surprise and his white head bobbed up and down with a greeting.

"Well, I'll be! Hello, Bert. Where did you come from? Pull up a chair. Sit a spell."

"Keep your voice down!" Bert said in a hoarse whisper.

"Huh?"

Bert grinned. "Nick, you're always talking about wanting to get in on a little action again."

"Sure enough!"

"I need your help. Are you ready to put your money where your mouth is?"

"What's going on?"

Bert briefed him and watched the old man's blue eyes light up with excitement.

"You can count on me, Bert! Yes sir, you sure can."

"All right. This is what I want to do. About dusk, I'll go down to the boat. You join me. We'll cruise around awhile, pretend to be fishing or something. We'll stay until dark and then, without running lights, we'll drift

175

toward a location directly out from the Bleaker house. Can you manage that without trouble?"

Nick cackled. "You know I can! Got the stars, ain't I? Enough lights on shore to guide me. I'll take you to any spot out there you want."

"Good," Bert said. "It may be dangerous."

"Ain't scared. Darned glad to be getting after those punks. But what can you do, Bert?"

"Maybe not much. But they'll have to come to the shore to unload their drugs. Probably disguise themselves as picnickers or something. While they're making the exchanges, I'll foul their boat someway. Anything to keep them from making their getaway—"

"Might not work."

"Maybe not. But I can't tackle them on shore. I'll have to do what I can on the water."

"Aye, aye, sir," Nick grinned. "We'll fix them."

"Sure," Bert said, breathing quickly. "We'll fix them!"

The rest of the day, Bert stayed hidden in Nick's quarters, wondering if he'd been wise in enlisting the old man's help. But he was sure he could trust Nick. He had a sure hand on the wheel and he could put the *Mary Belle* through her paces better than anyone.

Bert was too keyed up to sleep, even though he was still weary to the bone. Staying very quiet in the rooms over the garage, he heard Nick return from the airport with his father. If Dad knew what he was up to—Bert grinned. Dad would have a fit. Maybe he was sticking his neck out. But he was going to do it. He was going to put a crimp in Juan Gonzales that he wouldn't quickly forget!

It was dusk at last. Bert didn't know if Sutton would spot him or not, or even if the man was next door. That was just one of those risks he had to take.

He walked easily, almost leisurely down to the water. Then swiftly, he climbed aboard the *Mary Belle.* In a few minutes, Nick followed. Then, with a roar of the motor, they sped away. Bert looked back at Sea Mist. A hard knot of nerves settled in the pit of his stomach. Juan Gonzales was a dangerous man and so were his gang. Maybe he'd ought to have gone to the police. No.

They would have been swarming all over the Bleaker house and Juan was no fool, nor was Sutton. They would have been spotted, the delivery would have been postponed or moved to another location. It was best to do it alone. One small cabin cruiser on the Gulf wouldn't be suspect. He'd do what he could. If it wasn't enough—he sighed. Well, he would have tried. He would have at least had his own personal revenge.

"Nick, you sure you want to go through with this?" Bert asked.

The old man nodded vigorously.

"You betcha!"

He was as excited as a kid going to a birthday party.

Some party, Bert thought. It might be some party!

At the Flamingo Motel, Sutton was briefing his men.

"You all know your positions, your jobs?" he asked.

Monroe nodded slowly. "Yeah, we know, Sutton. You've told us a dozen times."

"Can't be too careful. We can't be spotted! That's imperative! There's too much at stake, too much work, too much time—"

Sutton rubbed the scars on his back, feeling the welts through his shirt. He was very tired. It had been a long way down the road coming to this point. A spasm was trying to ripple its way through his muscles. Going to the bathroom, he got a glass of water and took two of the capsules. It would be his luck to buckle up at the crucial moment. He was perspiring. He'd waited so long for this day, for this night, for this contact. He couldn't risk anything going wrong now. Especially himself!

He checked his pistol and looked about the room to his men.

"Is everyone ready?"

"Ready."

"Then I think we'd better go. It will be dark by the time we get there. Remember—caution. Use caution. We don't know who might be there waiting!"

They left the shabby Flamingo Motel and got into their separate autos. Sutton eased himself behind the wheel. His heart was thundering. Going like a triphammer. Normally on these jobs he was cool and calm.

But this one hadn't gone quite according to plan. There had been too many hitches, too many changes and worst of all, they'd let Bert Goodwin get away without really finding out what he knew.

"Let's go," Monroe said beside him. "What are you waiting for?"

"Nothing," Sutton murmured.

They drove away and Sutton shut out all other thoughts but the job ahead. In a few hours, it would all be over. He would be leaving Gull Haven.

The first act at the playhouse had ended more than twenty minutes ago. Lee was pacing like a man about to go mad and everyone in the cast had searched the premises for Nollie.

"Can't someone fill in?" Larina asked.

Lee stared at her as if she'd lost her mind. "Of course not! Nollie wouldn't have an understudy. I should have known better than let him talk me into that! He was never reliable. But where is he now? If I ever get my hands on that guy—"

There was a sudden, loud explosion. Everyone grew silent, staring at each other.

"What was that?" Larina asked, her hand going to her throat. "Lee—"

"Shots! Gunshots!" someone screamed. "Over at the Bleaker house. Hey, something's going on over there—"

XXII

INSTINCTIVELY, Larina knew what the shots were all about. The smugglers. Bert was out there somewhere in the boat, she was sure of it. Those shots—Bert— With a sense of terror, Larina ran from the playhouse. By now, everyone had heard the shooting and people came pouring out of the theatre.

"Larina! Larina!"

It was Uncle Ernie, shouting to her, telling her to stop. But there was no stopping her. She ran until the sand came up over the tops of her shoes. She paused only long enough to kick them off. There were sirens now, more shots, a man's scream.

Sutton? Was Sutton there? Had he been shot? Had he been caught receiving the drugs from the smugglers?

"Hold it, Miss. You can't go any farther!"

A man in a blue uniform had stopped her. But she tried to break free. He held tight.

"No, Miss. You can't go any closer. This is a police matter!"

"The smugglers? Have they caught the smugglers?"

"They sure have, Ma'am!"

She felt sick. Turning away, she saw Uncle Ernie running toward her. She went to meet him.

"Larina, are you all right? Larina—"

"Oh, Uncle Ernie, it's all so terrible. So terrible!"

"What are you talking about, Larina?"

Bert came jogging toward them. Uncle Ernie stared with surprise. "Bert! Where did you come from?"

"Out there," Bert said, pointing to the Gulf. "Nick and I took the *Mary Belle* out. We got in on the action. In fact, we turned out to be quite an asset in capturing the smugglers. How about that, Dad? Did you ever think your wayward son would become a hero?"

"Wait a minute. Back up. Explain—will you?"

"Oh, Bert, I'm so glad you're all right. I was so worried," Larina said.

"I'm fine. Got a little warm out there, but we got them!"

"The smugglers? They caught all the smugglers?"

"Red-handed. It's prison for them!"

Sutton! In prison. Sutton—the man she had fallen in love with was just a—a—criminal—

Larina had never fainted before in her life. But she did then.

When she opened her eyes, she was home at Sea Mist in her room, and Aunt Stell was bending over her.

"How do you feel now, dear?"

"Better," she murmured. "Where's everyone?"

"Bert's down at the station, making his statement. Your uncle went along. I can't believe it! Bert and Nick helping to capture the smugglers. Your uncle is so proud."

"Yes," Larina said tonelessly.

"They confiscated the drugs too! It was estimated that they were worth over a million dollars. The man in charge was Juan somebody or other. From Mexico."

Larina nodded. "I know."

"You know! How do you know?"

"It's a very long story. I'm so tired, Aunt Stell. I think I'll just go back to sleep."

"Yes. You do that. Mr. Tyler called. Wanted to know if you were all right."

"Too bad about the play. I guess it sort of ruined the opening."

"There'll be another," Aunt Stell said. "Now, try to get some rest, Larina."

Larina was glad when the door closed and she was alone. It was very late when she heard Uncle Ernie and Bert come home. Bert knocked at her door, but she pretended to be asleep. She couldn't talk about it. She couldn't hear all the sordid details. Not just yet. Her heart bled so much.

Oh, Sutton, Sutton, Sutton!

She fell into a fitful sleep at last. When she awakened, the sun was shining brightly. It was one of those golden Florida days. The beach stretched out white and smooth. The gulls cried with scratchy voices. The fishing boats went chugging out to sea. It was all so peaceful. So very, very peaceful. She sighed. Perhaps if Bert would promise to stay home for awhile, she could return to Riverdale immediately. She had come here determined to keep faith with John, only to learn that she didn't really love him. She had fallen in love with Sutton Ward instead!

Once she had told Dad that love knew no age, no reason, no season. But for a little while, this summer, it had been a season for love. Now—only disillusionment. A broken heart. A shattered faith.

She dressed and went downstairs. No one was about but Bertha.

"Good morning," Bertha said.

"Where is everyone?"

"Bert persuaded them to walk up the beach with him. He wanted to show them just how they captured the smugglers last night."

"I see."

"Will you have breakfast now?"

"Just some coffee, Bertha."

"I'll have it ready in a minute or two. Wasn't that something about Mr. Ward! Who would have thought it?"

Her heart gave a painful lurch. "Yes. It was quite a surprise wasn't it?"

"There was a telephone message for you. From the Home. They'd like you to come by this morning. Jimmy wants to see you."

"Oh, yes. I promised him I'd be there today. As soon as I have my coffee."

The coffee didn't taste good. She had no appetite for anything. But she drank two cups anyway to bolster herself for the day.

She was relieved to leave the house and drive to the Home. She wished that whoever had made the drugs available to Jimmy's mother had been caught in time. But they hadn't. Still, with Sutton and his men in prison, some of the drugs coming into the country illegally would be stopped.

When Jimmy saw her convertible turning in at the drive, he came running and she knew with one look that something had happened. He was positively glowing.

"Hello, Jimmy."

"Hello, Larina. You know what?"

"No," she laughed. "What?"

"They decided they liked me. Those people. They liked me! Tomorrow, I'm going to their house to live."

"What's this?"

He prattled on, words falling all over themselves. His eyes were dancing and she finally understood that the little boy had been adopted.

"Oh, Jimmy, I told you it would happen, didn't I?"

"I'm going to take my big seashell with me. They said I could."

She took his little face in her hands. "Bless you, Jimmy. Keep it to remember me by, will you?"

"I'll keep it forever and ever. Will you come visit me?"

"If I can," she promised. "But I expect I'll be going home soon. But I'll keep in touch. I'll write you big, long letters."

He gave her a hard, swift hug and for a moment, she held the little boy close.

"Jimmy, someone's going to be very lucky to have you!" she whispered.

She told him good-bye a few minutes later. He was being called inside. She watched him until he reached the door. There, he waved and gave her his big, bright grin. With a sigh, she waved back.

Driving home, she thought about Jimmy. He'd been lucky. He'd found new parents, a new home. She hoped it worked out for him.

Putting the convertible in the garage, she slipped around to her studio and hung out a little sign that said she didn't want to be disturbed. She knew the family would honor that. At the moment, she couldn't face them. Her heart was much too heavy, too crushed. She found the portrait of Sutton and stared at it. How could he have betrayed her like that? How could she have been so blind about him, so wrong?

She pushed the portrait out of sight. Why couldn't she bring herself to destroy it now this very minute?

In that very chair, Sutton had posed for her. On that divan, they had watched the rain together. Sutton had kissed her, so warmly, so gently. How could a man be like that and then turn out to be—a—drug smuggler!

Angrily, she set up her easel. She would work. She would paint. She would never, never think of Sutton Ward again.

But the work did not go well. After she'd spent an hour there, she decided she might as well give up. Just as she was putting her brushes away, she heard familiar steps outside her door. She froze with a sense of shock.

The door came open. He stood there, staring at her with gray eyes, his hair very black, a faint smile on his face.

"You!" she gasped.

"Me," he nodded.

"But how, I mean—aren't you in—"

"Jail?" he asked with amusement. "No. I'm not in jail. I just spoke with your cousin. He told me he hadn't talked with you since the arrests made last night. I assume he hasn't explained to you who I really am."

"What do you mean?"

He laughed easily and came into the room. Very deliberately, he sat down.

"My back's a little tired. You don't mind if I don't keep standing, do you?"

Her head was spinning.

"Sutton—"

He held up his hand. "Shall I begin at the beginning? I think I should. I told you one day soon I would tell you all about myself. Now, the time has come. My name is Sutton Ward. But I'm not a playboy. Never have been, never will be. I'm a special agent for the F.B.I. I work out of Washington."

Her mouth fell open with surprise. "Then you're not—"

"I'm not a criminal. No. Just the opposite. A few months ago, I tangled with Juan Gonzales. I took a couple of bullets in my back. I was lucky. I got out alive. The shots damaged some nerves. I do have a bad back. The scars aren't from a surgeon's incision, but just where the bullets were dug out of me."

"Oh, dear!"

"Well, I decided to get him. The boss didn't think it was wise, but I talked fast and persuaded him. So, I came down here. Of course, we had information that made us think the contact would be made at the Bleaker house."

"I'm not sure I understand, even now!"

"I spent most nights there, watching for the signal. There were some mix-ups. It was all set to go a few weeks ago and then something went wrong. Then your cousin arrived in town and I'm afraid we thought he was on their side."

"Bert!"

Sutton laughed. "Yes. We didn't know who he was and he didn't really know who we were. We wanted the information we thought he had. But he didn't trust us and we couldn't tell him we were the police. If he had been one of Juan's men as we mistakenly believed—it would have ruined everything if we'd tipped our hand."

"Yes, of course. I see! But who was the contact man?"

"You haven't heard?" Sutton asked with raised brows.

"No. I—I haven't wanted to listen to the news on the radio—I haven't seen the papers—"

"Nollie Oliver."

"Nollie!"

"He was late getting here. I understand he got jailed for a few days on a minor charge in another state. That's why the delivery didn't come off as scheduled."

"Nollie!"

"Nollie was the main contact. There were two others. Local men. I knew Nollie from another scrape with the law. I think he had me spotted, for he ducked meeting me face-to-face whenever he could. His job was to take the drugs and move them inland and farm them out to other contacts. Thanks to Bert and Nick's unexpected help, we got them all."

She was beginning to feel a little weak in the knees. "Oh, I've been so stupid, so blind—so—"

He laughed. "It's all right, Larina. I can't blame you for thinking the worst of me. I wanted to tell you, but I couldn't. You understand?"

"Yes," she nodded.

He got to his feet and walked stiff-legged to the door. Reaching around it and outside, he held out the painting of the studio.

"Tish had this in her window this morning. Were you so angry with me?"

Larina flushed. "I—I was—very unhappy."

He took the painting and put it back on her easel.

"Promise me that you'll never sell it," he said. "It's a very special painting, isn't it? You can make others for the Home."

"Oh, Sutton—"

He came to her and with a rush, he swept her into his arms. Then she was crying all over the front of his shirt and he was stroking her hair.

"I love you, Larina. Part of my life here had to be a sham but that part wasn't. It was real. Very, very real. I love you, Larina."

He lifted her tear-stained face.

"As I remember, we were interrupted a few nights ago. At a very crucial time. Will you be ready at seven thirty? We'll try again."

"All right, Sutton. All right!"

The rest of the day was one of happy confusion for Larina. Bert was basking in his new-found fame, Nick was strutting with importance and Uncle Ernie was as proud as a peacock of them both.

Lee was looking for someone to replace Nollie in the play. Angel was very much in evidence and Lee didn't seem to mind. The whole Beach Front Road was in a turmoil over the excitement. Then it was evening at last and Larina wore the same pink dress. Sutton called for her and they drove to the dock where the same yacht waited. Harry was there too and gave them a quick salute.

"Ready and waiting, Skipper."

"Shove off!" Sutton said with a grin.

The gulls followed them for a little while and then turned back. Soon, Gull Haven was behind them.

Everything was as before. Below, the food waited and the candles burned. The music flowed from the tape player. They dined leisurely, talking quietly, eyes meeting, hands touching.

Then they went up to the deck. The sunset was brilliant. The open sea was like black velvet, tinged with pink.

Harry had done the disappearing act. The boat rocked gently. Sutton came to Larina and pulled her into his arms.

"Now," he said. "Before we were so rudely interrupted, I believe I was asking you to marry me."

"So you were," she said with a happy smile.

"And your answer?"

She put her arms around his neck and lifted her lips to his for a long, warm kiss.

"My answer is yes. Oh, yes!"